DEEDS OF SALVATION

LANCE COLBERT SMITH

Deeds of Salvation

ISBN: 978-0-9945307-8-3

© 2020 Lance Colbert Smith

All rights reserved.

No part of this book may be used or reproduced in any manner whatsoever without the written permission of the author, except in the case of brief excerpts for review, study or promotional purposes.

Published in Australia by Rainbow Works Pty Ltd. Pottsville, NSW.

Cover design by Patrick Williams at the Petridish.

First Edition: October 2020

Disclaimer

Rainbow Works Pty Ltd is committed to publishing works of quality and integrity. In that spirit, we are proud to offer this book to readers; however, the story is entirely the author's creation.

This story is pure fiction. None of the events described happened as related, and the characters exist only in the author's imagination. Any resemblence to a real person is purely coincidental. A number of known historical figures are referred to by name—not as characters, but for the sole purpose of adding context to the story. The author has endeavoured to ensure accuracy in such references, but offers no assurance that all references are entirely factual.

Dedication

I dedicate this book to former Inspector John B and Maurean for all their wonderful support over the years, and to our beautiful all-Australian girl, Tania K.

Together we have blazed many trails.

PROLOGUE

Death has no boundaries. No particular time or place—and certainly no common cause. Death can visit anytime, anywhere, and in many ways.

Take a beautiful, peaceful Sunday morning in Vaucluse, Sydney. The calm seas lap the jagged rocks at the base of the spectacular gap. Not a cloud in the clear, aqua blue skies. Yachts of all shapes and sizes could be seen out at sea or rounding Hornby Lighthouse at South Head, all moving gracefully, gently nudged by a wispy breeze.

Two good friends sat in the morning sun at the footpath tables outside their local café, discussing the forthcoming nuptials of a favourite daughter at the nearby Our Lady Star of the Sea Catholic Church.

Jim Davis and his mate, Pab Gonzalez, were sipping coffee and going through the guest list. Jim's daughter was the apple of dad's eye, and he so wanted the day to go well. He was smiling at the thought.

An elderly couple strolled past, walking their dog, holding hands and laughing, probably headed down the hill to Watsons Bay or, maybe, Robertson Park.

A sleek, silver BMW travelled slowly down the road towards them, obviously looking for a car space—always difficult on a Sunday morning, especially on such a perfect day. It came to a stop outside the café, just as both front and back windows slid smoothly open.

'Wipeout' smiled.

The silence of the morning was shattered by the sound of automatic machine gun fire coming from both windows, quickly followed by the screeching of tyres as the BMW sped off in a cloud of smoke and disappeared down Marine Parade. It was all over in seconds.

There would be no wedding day for Jim or Pablo. Their bullet-ridden bodies lay on the footpath with blood flowing into the gutter.

Then the screaming started…

CHAPTER ONE

Tina:

Detective Chief Inspector, Tina Samuels, squinted as she emerged into the sunlight from the Sydney Metro underground at Chatswood Station. She reflected that it had been a prudent move to purchase the Epping unit four years earlier, so close to the station.

The new train service runs every few minutes to the Police Missing Persons HQ, just up from Chatswood Railway Station, and hubby, David, does most of his design work at home. Works well for both of them.

Tall, with short fair hair, an attractive, strong face and piercing stare, Tina was a force to be reckoned with.

The twenty-four-hour break had been her first day off in just over a month—since the Riley Sampson case began. She had needed it.

As Tina strode along Victoria Street, her mind focused back on the job at hand and the apparent abduction. She reached the foyer and quickly cleared security.

"Morning, Sir," a cheeky greeting from Bryce Rixon, the Desk Sergeant.

Tina waved back, smiling at the number of her task force that called her 'Sir'." Didn`t worry Tina. She was pleased to have been promoted to Chief Inspector last year.

By and large, she was happy with her ten strong 'Taskforce Delta' team. They were a terrific crew—certainly skilful and hard working. They needed more, of course, but pressures from above prevented any expansion.

Today, Tina had scheduled a ten a.m. meeting with the whole team, to go over their progress before she submitted her latest report to Police Commissioner Palmer tomorrow. She had made herself a strong, black coffee—her standard routine—and headed into her office.

"Hey, Boss, can I have a quick word with you?" It was Tina's right-hand man, Mike Broadfinger, a smart, well-respected Detective Sergeant she had worked with for many years. Tina motioned him to sit down.

Mike settled his tall, fit frame and basketballer's shoulders into the chair and tossed the *Daily Telegraph* to her. "Page eleven," he said, "Our mole has been at it again."

The headlines claimed, "Sampson Kidnapping Case in chaos." It went on to say there was infighting and disagreement within the Taskforce Delta ranks. Loosely, it was correct. There were many opinions about a number of suspects and about the value of a number of leads and groundwork. That was normal in these cases.

"Whoever it is, they have to be in the inner circle. We've got a rat in the ranks."

Tina agreed and sighed. "We need this like a hole in the head. Day Street HQ is riding us for results, and this will make them even more concerned. Any ideas?"

Mike was at a loss. "I'm buggered if I can think of anyone. What's in it for them?"

Tina's eyes narrowed as though stung by betrayal. "Is everyone here for the meeting?"

"No. Bruno is on surveillance. I've got his file. Everyone else is here."

"Right, give me half an hour to go over the latest and then come back."

"Sure thing. By the way, how was the day off?"

"Slept in. A medical check-up and dinner with David at the Epping RSL. Not much else, but I did enjoy it."

By ten, everyone was in the well-appointed briefing room, pouring over the many case notes on the walls and white boards. When everyone was settled, Tina opened, "First up, thanks for downing tools to go over this again. I need to be bought up to speed as Commissioner Palmer is breathing down my neck. He's not a happy chappy, as he is being hounded by both the Minister and the media. My immediate concern, though, is how another story has appeared in today's papers, and it seems to have come from this room. Before I go to Riley's case let me say this—just once. If someone here has a problem with our work or me, come and have it out. There will be no grudges or retribution, and my door is always open to any of you. ***But...*** if I find out someone here is undermining me or any other member of our team, in any way, behind our backs, they will wish I had only fired them!"

Tina let that sink in. She had overheard two of them talking a few weeks earlier. "I think she's got balls," one of them had said. Tina didn`t mind. That is a mark of respect in a man's world. She turned her thoughts to the Sampson case, mulling over events from day one of the investigation.

Riley Sampson was just seven years old and had disappeared from a school bush camp at Narrabeen Lakes nearly five weeks earlier, sometime after nine-ish in the morning. No one saw or heard anything out of place, and Riley had said nothing to any of his friends. He wasn't reported missing until mid morning, when he had not been seen with his group since breakfast and had not participated in any of the camp activities.

The group leaders were devastated. Riley was a very popular kid. No one had a clue about what had happened to him.

As news broke SES and volunteers, camp staff and police had searched all the area and surrounding bush land, and police divers had carried out a thorough search of the lakes themselves. Nothing.

There were possible sightings of a boy fitting Riley's description in nearby Brookvale, on the Wakehurst Parkway, at Seaforth—even one at Taronga Zoo. None of them produced any concrete leads. Riley's mum, Jan, was beside herself with worry. A single mum, living at Hornsby with her folks, she worked at the nearby Westfield Plaza. As the days went on, she became increasingly distraught and was causing quite a bit of concern, particularly for her mental wellbeing.

Enquiries soon established Jan and her husband, Rick Sampson, had split some eighteen months earlier. He was a successful real estate agent, working and living at his own business at West Pennant Hills. His movements and whereabouts on the day had been carefully checked and cleared.

Motives were scarce, and the usual round-up of all known paedophiles in the district had produced nought to date. The Taskforce Delta team had checked out all the camp staff, Riley's regular school teachers from Normanhurst State School, and all his extended family members from both sides.

Inspector Samuels threw to Mike Broadfinger. "Sergeant, did you get any further with the team leader, Alan Trundle?" she asked

"Well, he does have a serious gambling problem and is in deep financial shit, but we've had no ransom requests, nor found anything in his past that would point the finger at anything worse."

There were a few murmurs, as some of the team were convinced Trundle was a creep. He had certainly lied about his gambling problems when first questioned.

"What about the catering delivery? Any progress?" asked Tina.

"Nothing unusual from the company, but the young driver said he noticed a snazzy light-blue Mercedes convertible parked just off the entry road in the bush. It had gone before he left, around nine-forty-five," reported the ever-zealous Detective Constable Georgia McHenry. "I am looking further into it."

Georgia was short in stature with attractive features, and was a popular, switched on team member. She was due to be married in just under two months.

"Brian, anything more from the extended families?" Tina asked undercover Detective Carey.

"One of the uncles from Riley's dad's side, 'Bushy' Thompson, is a small-time mobster with the Cobama Gang around Parramatta. He has a record of petty crime, but nothing like this. That's about it from both sides."

Tina liked Carey. He never stood out but had great respect from everyone and a valuable network of contacts in the underworld.

Brad Henderson spoke up. "One of the camp office staff reported a phone call just after nine, from an anonymous person advising they had seen two suspicious characters loitering in the thick bush near the western boundary of the complex. They sent three people to check it out, but found nothing, but Riley had not been reported missing then."

Tina was not sure about Brad. He seemed to have a bee in his bonnet over many of their recent group decisions and was not displaying team spirit. This wasn't like him. He certainly was not his normal smiling self.

The meeting broke up around 10.45 a.m., with nothing new or major coming out of the various reports. Tina had returned to her office to go over all the files. She was convinced they must have overlooked something small but important, and she was desperate to solve what appeared to be an abduction. Tina was terrified it could happen again on her watch. They had no idea if Riley was alive or dead. No ransom demands had been made—and that's a bad sign. Her vibrating mobile brought her out of her trance. She looked at the screen, frowned, then answered, "Morning, Commissioner."

"Samuels, I have just had a call from the Minister. He is getting very agitated with our lack of progress on the Riley Sampson case and pissed off with today's newspaper coverage. What's going on? It seems like this case is going nowhere."

"We're doing our best, Sir. There is a mass of information and leads coming in from all sides, but nothing turning up trumps. I have no idea who it is leaking to the media, but I am moving on that as we speak. Sorry I can't offer any better news."

Commissioner John Palmer was tall, distinguished and imposing. He liked Tina and held her in high esteem.

"Samuels, watch your back. It seems someone is out to get you. That report due tomorrow—I want it this afternoon." And then he hung up.

Tina's shoulders slumped a little. She wondered if her uncovering of internal corruption was coming back to haunt her. She was under way more pressure than she wanted and had no answers.

First, she called Mike Broadfinger into her office and told him she had a plan to catch 'the leak'. She had to trust someone, and she was certain she could trust Mike with her life. "I want to see Brad Henderson at two p.m., Graham James at two-thirty, and Jim Heggarty at three, and I want you to follow up on the Parramatta mobster lead. I think that's the Moriarty mob. See if you can join the dots to anyone else involved."

Mike left, and Tina started work on her updated report, scanning every file. What had she missed?

Around three-thirty p.m., the desk phone rang. Her PA advised it was a Dr Marie Emslie from the San Hospital.

"Good afternoon Dr Emslie," said Tina to her favourite oncologist.

"Good afternoon, Tina. I have just received your scans from yesterday. There are a couple of things we need to address. I would like to see you first thing in the morning, here at the San. Is nine-thirty okay?"

"Is there something wrong?" asked Tina. "I am in the middle of a major case here, but I can make it if you think I must."

"Okay. I'll see you at nine-thirty ," said Dr Emslie.

What now? thought Tina. *Whatever it is I don't need it.*

The commissioner's report was emailed just before four p.m., after a few quick meetings with the three team members. Tina knew it did not answer any of the Minister's concerns. She needed a breakthrough.

Just then, Broadfinger burst into her office. "Boss, another kid missing. Close to where Riley lives! Sounds similar to Riley, same age, apparently abducted from Pennant Hills about half an hour ago. I think we had better get out there."

They both left the office in a hurry. Tina crossed her fingers as they sped along the Comenarra Parkway towards Pennant Hills.

Chapter Two

Alvaro

He awoke with a start—instantly alert. The bedside clock showed 3:12 a.m. Alvaro was sweating… more bad dreams. His mind wandered.

Alvaro Pedro Palez loved Australia and wanted to do more for it. He had been here almost eight years, having taken over five years and three refugee camps to achieve his goal, but he was on his third Temporary Protection Visa (TPV) and feared it may be his last.

His thoughts went back to that stormy night they came ashore on Christmas Island. How they made it in that stinking, leaking, overcrowded excuse for a boat he will never know. But there they were—and alive!

The Australian asylum-seeking interviews were harrowing for Alvaro, even though he had been well briefed in Jakarta and later in Lombok. He had no papers but knew what to say. Indonesia had become a transit hub for refugees, but they had never signed the International Refugee Convention Agreement and so did not guarantee any basic human rights.

Alvaro had many nightmares about life in his homeland, Colombia: the murders, the mass killings and the armies controlled by the drug lords. He had been a successful up-and-coming lawyer. He was a member of the powerful Sarmiento family. His cousin was one of the five presidential candidates murdered by the drug cartels for standing up to them. This was a terrible blow to the whole family, and they were living in fear.

Corruption was rife. Eleven of the twenty-five Supreme Court Magistrates had been assassinated in the last two years, and a number of those remaining had 'protection' from the mobs in return for regular judicial 'favours'. But Colombia did have many decent politicians and citizens trying to overcome organised crime. In 1988, they had signed the 'Vienna Convention against the Illegal Traffic of Narcotic Drugs and Psychotropic Substances Agreement.' They had aggressively worked to achieve their aims.

There were four major drug cartels and hundreds of splinter mobs, all vying for territory in this insidious trade. The 'Bandas Criminales', or 'Bacrim', was well known and constantly pursued by the authorities. The wars between the FARC Guerrillas and other groups had almost bought the country to its knees, with all of them trying to gain a bigger share of the estimated $7 billion annual illicit drug trade. Trade was mainly to the USA, where a recent survey showed one in every six adults had experimented with cocaine, but also to Australia, Asia, UK and Europe, where their criminal gangs were well established and operating. The capture and death of Pablo Escobar, head of the feared Madellin Cartel, had sent warnings to the remaining gangs that the authorities were closing in.

Many of the Madellin members had rolled over as a plea bargain for a lighter sentence. Colombian gaols are feared. The Southern Colombian Cali Cartel, also, was happy to assist, as the Madellin mob had been expanding south recently.

Alvaro's older brother, Gresco, had played a major role in catching Escobar but was murdered soon after in a horrific bomb blast that also killed seven of his colleagues. Retribution, Colombian style.

Alvaro remembered his parents and sisters in total shock and disbelief. The wailing and tears went on for days after Gresco's funeral in Barranquilla. Gresco was among hundreds of honest journalists, officials, politicians and police massacred that year. That was the main reason Alvaro decided to dedicate the rest of his life to bringing the cartel ringleaders to justice.

Alvaro remembered how proud his parents were when he had opened his legal practice in Bogota. As a young lawyer, he was making quite a name for himself—a name he would soon bury, as they had buried his brother. He quickly became a valuable ally to those fighting against organised crime.

During the first few years, Alvaro established a large network of cartel members who sought his legal services. He became a trusted confidante of many key underworld players.

Alvaro was amazed how well he was balancing his legal practice and home life—with his beautiful Spanish born wife Olga and their two wonderful, much-loved children, Rodriguez and Zarla—as well as his undercover liaison with his two senior, honest police contacts. He *was* making a difference.

Alvaro was happy that his vital information had already led to the arrest, conviction and gaoling of a number of cartel ringleaders. Then one morning, out of nowhere, he was shattered. He received an urgent call on his private phone from his Assistant Police Commissioner contact. All he heard was. "Bernardo, get out quick. They are on to us," and then the volley of shots and the screaming.

Alvaro remembered quickly ringing Olga and yelling, "Get the children *now!* Go to your parents in the country *now.* Don't wait one second!" He recalled running down to the nearby Banque Nationale de Paris, where he was well-known, and withdrawing US$40000 from his trust funds 'for a real estate settlement'. Standard practice.

He had decided not to use his own car so caught a taxi to the airport. Along the way he heard graphic breaking-news reports on the radio of the assassination of two senior police officers in Bogota headquarters that morning.

The next few years were hell.

In one of the camps, he made friends with a like-minded Colombian his own age. They shared many deep and meaningful conversations. Sadly, his new friend, Alvaro Padro Palez, drowned in a tragic attempted refugee-boat crossing. He had no papers on him, nor any identification.

Bernardo—as he still was—decided he needed a new identity, as he would be chased by the Colombian mobsters. A 'new' Alvaro Padro Palez moved on to the next camp. 'Alvaro' felt safer with his new name.

The UNHCR in Indonesia by now had over 13,000 people registered for refugee status on their books. Alvaro was not amongst them.

But, later, facing Australian immigration officers on Christmas Island and their determined questioning, he was aware that, even if he gets his TPV, 'Alvaro' was not likely to qualify for full refugee status.

He was well aware that his real name and identity would qualify him. But, equally he knew, the organised crime gangs would soon get wind of his arrival and he would be dead within hours. There would be a time. The mobs never forgot, nor forgave. They were forever trying to set 'examples', and were ruthless.

For those first five years in Asia, Alvaro had agonised over the fate of his beautiful Olga and much-loved children. He prayed daily for their good health, prosperity and survival without knowing a thing. He had sent only one coded message in all the years he had been away—an innocuous tourist postcard from Bali sent to Olga's parents, giving no details other than he was doing well. He had signed it 'Tagar', which was the crazy nickname Olga had given him on their honeymoon. He knew she would recognise it straight away, but no one else would.

His early days on Christmas Island, and later at Villawood Detention Centre in Sydney, were certainly better than the Indonesian camps, but he still felt like a caged animal and longed to establish himself in the 'free world'.

Early work was difficult because his visa restrictions prevented him from getting a real job and paying taxes. He was forced, along with many others, to accept underpaid cash-in-hand jobs like labouring, dish washing and varying menial tasks—often between $7-$10 per hour and, equally often, unpaid hours. There was no one to complain to.

Alvaro had been working at a car wash at Parramatta, when he was told by one of his close friends of a good opening, with proper wages, at the Sydney fruit and vegetable markets. Using his friend's contacts, he was successful. That had started a much improved next five years.

During this time, Alvaro shifted into a small but neat, tastefully appointed bed-sitter in Annandale. He had already made many good friends and had become one of the most respected volunteers at a number of local charities nearby. He was contributing on many levels and gaining valuable knowledge and associations.

One day, his long-time boss and good friend, 'Nick the Greek', took him aside at the markets. "Hey Alvaro, you are Colombian yes?"

Alvaro nodded, so Nick went on, "Then I tell you good advice. Stay away from that Carlos Carezo in the market administration office. He is a bad man and working for the Columbian Bandas Criminales."

Alvaro was shaken to the core. "Why are you telling me this?" he asked.

Nick's reply sobered him up. "I have got to know you well over the past four years. You are a good man whose intelligence is wasted here. You are hiding something, so I tell you as a friend."

Over the next twelve months, Alvaro picked up many more snippets of mob information by asking questions of people he trusted, without giving anything away. Life was frustrating him. Alvaro could not see a clear path ahead. He had gathered so much intelligence but, also, too much to lose if he told the wrong people. He knew he had to be careful and patient. One day, he was sure he would find a way and something good would happen. He just needed to find a way of contacting Olga safely.

CHAPTER THREE

Detective Chief Inspector Tina Samuel's dread echoed in the screaming siren as she and her 2IC drove to Pennant Hills Primary School to investigate a possible abduction of an eight-year-old boy. Mike drove. Tina was on the phone.

Reports were that eight-year-old Blair Chambers had gone missing just after three-thirty p.m. He was last seen with some classmates heading to the pickup area in Ramsay Road. It appears Blair's mother was a few minutes late and had raised the alarm with the 'Lollypop Lady' children's crossing attendant.

"Get the mother's address and check with DOCS to see if there is any history. We'll be there in about five minutes," Tina had instructed the local officer in charge at the scene.

"You're almost home," Mike observed.

Tina's mind had wandered momentarily as she pondered the call from her doctor asking her to be at the San Hospital tomorrow morning. They were just driving past the hospital turn off now. She snapped back to the task at hand. "I wish," she responded. "But this could be another late night. Whatever you do, keep young Riley's case in your thinking to see if there is a link."

There was pandemonium as they pulled in: parents running to check on their charges; teachers, police, media, even an ambulance, plus the usual throng of onlookers.

As she jumped from the car, Tina saw her Delta colleague, Georgia McHenry, heading towards her. "Hi, Chief. I was in Thornleigh when the call came in. I just need to tell you that I spoke to Blair's head teacher. She tells me she has been concerned about marks that appear to be burns and bruising on the youngster over the past couple of weeks. She hasn't flagged it yet but was keeping an eye on him. She says Blair is a good kid but does get down at times."

Tina thanked Georgia and asked to speak to Blair's mum. She was introduced to Cathy Chambers, who appeared to be no older than mid-20s.

"I've already told the officers. Blair can be a bugger at times, and it wouldn't surprise me if he's just gone down to the shops to buy lollies. I was a few minutes late, and he had gone before I arrived."

A police constable standing behind her shook his head, indicating Blair was not at the shops.

"Cathy, is there any reason Blair would run away from something or someone?"

Cathy Chambers immediately went on the defensive. "What are you implying?" she said. "He gets really well looked after at home."

"I'm not implying anything, Mrs Chambers. I am merely trying to rule out one thing at a time. Did Blair indicate he was being bullied or had troubles with anyone here at the school?"

"No."

"Has he disappeared before?" asked Tina.

"Not for long. Sometimes he wanders off to the park or the shops."

"Is Blair's dad at home or working?"

"Neither. He disappeared years ago. I have had a steady partner for the past five years. He's between jobs at the moment and at home," replied Cathy Chambers.

"Just on the off chance, does Blair have a friend named Riley Sampson?"

"He plays junior soccer for West Penno Tigers with a Riley. I don't know his surname. I think he goes to school at Castle Hill."

Tina noted this. She wondered if there was any connection as she made her way to the school admin block. Detective McHenry was moving towards her with a uniformed Sergeant Tina did not know.

"Sgt Bell says DOCS have been involved with the family but nothing serious—just following up calls from neighbours about kids home alone and a few minor domestic issues," reported Georgia. "But… better news. One of Blair's classmates thinks he saw him getting into another kid's car. We are onto it. We think it is a family he knows from Brush Farm."

"Oh God, I hope so," said Tina as she was escorted into the Principal's office to introduce herself.

Carole Barrymore was in her mid-fifties with grey hair, and looked very upset. "Inspector, I've been here fifteen years and nothing like this has ever happened before."

"We are still hopeful of a good ending Mrs Barrymore. Tell me, do you know young Blair?"

"Oh yes. He's a good boy. I think he struggles a bit at home. His Mum has a long-term partner and I don't think Blair is too fond of him. But there have been no reports of any serious troubles. He is well liked here at school by staff and students alike. I do hope he is okay."

Just then, Georgia came rushing in. "Drama over, Chief. Blair has just been located. He got a lift with a classmate's mum. He told her he was going to his grandmother's house in Kissing Point Road. She had taken him there before. We found him there. All is okay. They are bringing him back here now." Georgia smiled. "It seems like he just didn't want to go home."

The tension in the principal's office immediately dissipated.

"Mrs Barrymore, this happens all too often, I'm afraid. We need to get Blair and his mum—with her partner— on board and see if we can help them."

"Oh, Inspector, we have a wonderful councillor here who adores Blair and gets on well with his mum. I will make sure that happens and get back to you."

"Thanks, Mrs Barrymore. We are all very relieved."

As Tina got back into the police car, she said to Mike, "Thank goodness for that. If only they all ended up this way. You know what? I *am* nearly home, and it is after five. Drop me at the unit please, and I will see you mid morning tomorrow. I've something to do in the morning."

"Okay boss," he replied.

Tina had a restless night.

Chapter Four

Garth

The *Financial Review* headlines revealed, "Australian Wheat Board CEO at war with Chairman." The article went on to report that CEO Garth Peterson was allegedly not supporting the board's decision in relation to silo storage of surplus grain stocks and also the payment systems—particularly with Middle East contracts.

"Good luck, Garth," wished his deputy Evelyn Goldsmith as he headed towards the boardroom for what everyone knew was to be the showdown.

Chairman Bob Leeson opened the meeting pointing out the board's major challenge, with over-supply of many grain crops, along with shrinking sales prices and orders. He went on to say how disappointed he was that the CEO appeared to be speaking out publicly against the board's direction.

Leeson reminded them that they had lobbied long and hard in Canberra to get bipartisan support for Government purchases of excess grain supplies, at reasonable prices, to keep the industry afloat. He also said everyone knew that when doing business in the Middle East, it was common for invoice payments to be split to accommodate 'commissions' for second and third parties involved in the original trade negotiations. He also pointed out that many livelihoods were under threat.

"It is disappointing to see our CEO having problems with our success," said Leeson.

All eyes were immediately on Garth, who responded strongly with, "Mr Chairman, I have no problems whatsoever with the industry surviving and shoring up our sustainability, and I'm well aware of the plight of many rural communities. I do, however, have misgivings about paying separate silent commissions to multiple individuals as part of the negotiating process, and with bypassing Government instrumentalities.

I have also pointed out that our research shows that in our haste to acquire storage space for excess grain, we run a real risk of major long-term spoiling by using substandard facilities, which potentially could cost the Government millions of dollars in wastage.

"And I am also uncomfortable that the *Financial Review* continues reporting on information that must come from this room. Let me assure all of you, it does not come from me." Garth's firm gaze went directly into the eyes of all present. He had a deal of respect from the many board members who had been part of his success to date.

At this point all eyes went back to Bob Leeson, a politically-appointed chairman who did not enjoy one hundred percent respect from a number of the nine board members. Some saw him as a 'party stooge'. It was no secret he disliked the CEO, whom he saw as a barricade to his own future endeavours.

"Ladies and Gentleman, it is prudent for us to ensure the survival of many hundreds of rural and remote families and organisations currently under threat. I would also point out that, rather than worrying about the source of the media reports, I am more concerned with their accuracy. I am now going to ask the CEO to leave the meeting to allow us to have a private discussion."

With that, Garth left the room and returned to his office, feeling very unsure of his future. He was surprised to see a personal message from the chairman of one of Australia's largest public companies on his desk. Just three words: "Please ring me". He thought he would—but later, when things settled down.

It was early afternoon when the wheat board chairman came into Garth's office. "You would be well aware that many of the board members are not happy with your performance. I am here to advise you to think long and hard about your future which, I believe, will depend on you supporting and carrying out board decisions." With that, he stood straight up and strode out.

Garth was relieved. It could have been worse. But what now?

Deputy CEO Evelyn Goldsmith was quickly in the room.

"Well?" she asked.

Garth gave her details of both the board meeting and the chairman's advice.

"So what do we do?" asked Evelyn, who had tremendous respect for Garth, both as a person and a CEO. He had taught her well over the years.

"To be quite honest, I don't know. I'm going home to think about it and talk it over with Meg. First up, I am well aware that at least five of the forty-one silo sites we have secured for storage are nowhere near industry standards and present a real chance of inflicting long-term disasters with grain rot. I am also concerned that all five of those deals were personally negotiated by the chairman, at what I believe to be inflated prices.

Secondly, I truly believe the underhanded payments to individuals involved in our overseas trade negotiation will come back to haunt us in time, even if they do say they are legitimate commissions," he told Evelyn.

Later, Garth rang Rob Champion, one of his trusted board members, and organised to meet at the Golden Sheaf Hotel at Double Bay—a favourite watering hole for grain industry executives. He would tell Rob his misgivings.

Driving along New South Head Road, Garth reflected on his career to date. He was pleased with his academic achievements—dux at college, two honour degrees in advanced mathematics at university, graduating as a statistical scientist. His acceptance as a biometrician at the Wheat Board was immediate and his rise to CEO at just thirty-four—the youngest CEO by far—was well deserved, and came from results over a stellar twelve-year career of good decision-making and management. But now he was at a crossroad.

Over a few beers, Rob Champion, the Outback Qld. member of the board, outlined the events following Garth's departure from the meeting. "Leeson called for your head. He said it was only you standing in the way of a successful resolution to all of our industry challenges and glory for our board. It was a fiery couple of hours of heavy discussion. Leeson was livid when his motion went down five to four in a secret ballot."

Rob Champion had a distinguished track record in local Government and kindred organisations and was well-respected as a straight shooter. Garth certainly looked up to him. He smiled as he imagined the annoyance Leeson would have felt losing the motion and his chance to get rid of his nemesis. He drove home in a better frame of mind. At least he had the support of a slim majority of the board, but life would still be tough. He and Meg talked late into the night.

The next few years of Garth's life had been hectic and productive. First, he had followed up the unexpected phone message from the chairman of CRC, whom he had only met once before when negotiating storage space for grain. It was obvious he must have impressed him at the time. After much deliberation, Garth had accepted a lucrative contract offer and resigned from the Wheat Board, moving to Brisbane to head up a section of the new group, which was under performing. The media had a field day. In his first week he had crunched the numbers meticulously, and soon realised the two major obstacles facing the group were poor productivity and overbearing union influence on the operation, with many stoppages causing major losses. After a thorough briefing from all section managers, he called in the union chiefs to discuss their ongoing demands. He knew their request for a twenty-eight percent wage increase over three years, plus a number of extra perks, were just ambit claims—a high starting point—and that they would be prepared to come down. But what then?

Garth's management briefings had revealed many cumbersome, nonviable operational procedures which the unions had refused to allow to be changed. This was costing millions over and above the regular strikes and stoppages. A week after their first meeting Garth reconvened—this time with his full management team and all the union heavies in one room.

He advised the union representatives, "We are happy to negotiate your full list of demands, including the twenty-eight percent wage increase over three years, provided that you work with us to reduce operational waste costs and poor work practices by twenty percent, and agree in writing to refrain from any industrial stoppages for the next three years."

The unions were astonished and happy to co-operate in any way for such a huge pay rise. Garth gave them a full list of the required areas of improvement. Within seven days, agreement was reached, and within twelve months the worst performing area of the company had turned into the best. Garth's star was on the rise. Over the next few years, he was invited to head up many high-profile boards and organisations. The world was his oyster. His success also allowed him to indulge in his passion of breeding world-class equine stock, mainly for international dressage competitions, but also for racing.

Then, following his second year of successful stud-livestock auctions, Garth noticed that his urine was changing colour—first to a dark brown and later reddish brown. He ignored it for a couple of weeks and said nothing to Meg, not wanting to frighten her. Finally, he went to his GP, who referred him to a prominent urologist. After a number of scans and tests he was diagnosed with a high grade, aggressive bladder cancer that had already penetrated three layers of his muscle tissue. After all his success and achievements, his world was about to turn upside down.

Meg was distraught. She kept thinking of all their great achievements. What would happen now?

Chapter Five

Catie

Catie was mesmerised by the reflections of the candles on the rippling waters of the El Alamein Fountain in Kings Cross.

It was July 4th, 2019. The candles had been lit as a tribute—not to America's Independence Day, but to the memory of a well-known and fiercely independent investigative journalist, Juanita Nielsen, who had disappeared from the Cross in July 1975. Juanita had been a thorn in the side of shonky developers, crooked cops and corrupt politicians, and was last seen at the Carousel Club— the old Les Girls—on that fateful day. She had gone there for a meeting and was never seen again.

As a high profile and very successful anticorruption investigative journalist herself, Catie Lanyon was well aware that she faced many of the same threats and dangers that apparently bought Juanita's life to a premature end. She felt uneasy.

In 1983, the coroner had determined that Juanita 'was probably killed,' and also noted that 'police corruption may have crippled the investigation into her death'.

You can say that again, mused Catie to herself at the time. Her stomach had knotted again when she thought about how, three years later, Sallie-Anne Huckstepp's body was dragged out of the lake at Centennial Park, strangled. Sallie Anne was a part-time prostitute, a writer, and also a whistle-blower. You don't cross the mob.

Once again, the same old names were in the media: crooked cops, gang leaders, and, all too predictably, once again the police had plenty of leads but no results. No one was surprised. That's just the way it was.

Catie, though, was scared. Her editors at World News Inc. were aware that she was onto something huge. Her reputation for excellent I.T. knowledge and skills, and for bringing down the big guys— with meticulous research from her long list of reliable contacts—was already legendary. But this was way bigger than anything she had done previously, and who could she trust at work?

She knew some of her colleagues were pally with the organised crime hoods who were keen to get her information and sources. The brutal double murders of drug dealers Jimmy Davis and Pablo Gonzales, at Vaucluse last month, were still big daily news. Once again, the police were reporting many leads but no progress. Sydneysiders were becoming jumpy with all these gangland killings. But Catie knew all about them. She knew who the murderers were, and how the murders happened. She also knew, positively, who ordered the killings and who was protecting them. But who could she tell… and stay alive?

Catie had been surprised, last week, to get a late night urgent public phone-box call. An hour later, just after midnight, she opened her apartment door to let in a very nervous Anita Collins, former playboy model and now girlfriend of 'Wipeout' Tony Morabito, the hit man of the Moriarty gang.

"I was going to offer you a cuppa, but, by the look of it, you might want something stronger." Catie saw the bruises and cracked lips on Anita's face. Right now, Anita was a long way from the glamorous model Catie once knew.

Catie liked Anita. Although both attractive, they were very different. The two girls had a deal of respect for each other's roles and had spent some time together over the past few years. They got on well. Last year, Anita had asked Catie to be godmother to her first born—a little girl. Catie thought it over long and hard, but as she was no fan of Tony's, she gracefully declined.

"A cuppa would be fine. It's been a long day. Do you have any Milo?"

They enjoyed small talk for a while. Anita seemed to settle. The heater and hot drink did the trick.

Catie broke the ice. "You look like you have gone ten rounds with Mike Tyson. I hope that's not the norm in your life?"

"Well, put it this way. It's no real surprise, especially if Tony is really uptight," answered Anita. "But, no, it is not a common occurrence."

"Can I ask what has upset him this time?"

"He's got a price on his head. One million dollars—dead," said Anita flatly.

"Oh God! That is serious cash. Who is offering the money?"

"The Cobama Gang. There is a big drug turf war going on at the moment. Tony's mob took out Davis and Gonzalez last month in Vaucluse, and they are seeking revenge—payback. And that's just the start. I rang my mum on Monday in Brisbane. We used to be close but have sort of drifted apart over the past few years. We talked about the good old days, and I told her I did have some regrets but I was now too far in to bail out. Her response was that many people would say that I have made my own bed and had to lie in it, but she disagreed. She told me she had never stopped loving her 'feisty, funny, cuddly tomboy' and always knew that I had the courage and strength to stand up for myself. God, I hope she's right."

"From what I've always seen, I'm sure she's right," Catie assured her.

"Oh, thanks. I made up my mind to talk to the only outsider I trust: you. But you are the last person I want to put in danger." But the look in her eyes was saying help, *please*.

Catie came back with, "Don't worry about me. Danger is part of my everyday life."

"I do know that. You've been mentioned a number of times in the meetings the boys have in our billiard room at home."

For the next half-hour, Anita outlined her poor choices and the names, roles, murders, threats, major drug shipment details, crooked police, 'friendly' politicians and more. With Anita's blessing, Catie was madly taking notes.

Anita had explained the Moriarty operation and the tie up with the Colombian criminals. She gave Catie some of the names of those on the current hit list. Catie knew there were some good people on that list, including some of her close media associates and colleagues.

"Am I on that list?" asked Catie with some apprehension.

"Yes," was Anita's reply, as her sad eyes dropped to the floor.

"Christ," Catie retorted, and they talked more. After assuring Catie she would be okay, Anita left knowing Catie was going to sleep on it and work out a plan. But Catie couldn't sleep.

Around three a.m. she got up for a hot shower, hoping it would help. As the steam rose, Catie suddenly stifled a yelp. That small lump she had felt in her left breast last week was now much larger and more solid. Now she had two good reasons not to sleep, but she tried anyway.

Catie dragged herself out of bed just after seven thirty and toyed with black tea and fruit toast before making two important calls. The first was to her trusted oncologist. She could see her at ten. And the second was to her big boss at the paper. They arranged lunch for one p.m. at the Sydney Sports Club—the old journo's club. Safe territory.

CHAPTER SIX

Tina was shattered. Tears welled in her eyes. She had not seen this coming. She had never smoked! *Why me?*

"How sure are you?" she asked the doctor.

"Fairly sure," replied Marie Emslie "but we won't know for certain until we do the MRI scan." There are a number of spots in both lungs and, no, you don't have to be an active smoker to get lung cancer."

Dr. Emslie knew her long-time friend had never smoked and correctly guessed this was the reason for the quizzical look in her eyes. It was times like this that medical professionals wished they didn't know the patient so well.

"I could not get you a place until Friday at eight a.m. It will take up to two hours. The most important thing at the moment is not to fret. Firstly, we don't yet know what we are dealing with but, most importantly, whatever it is, we are in the early stages and our success with treatments is improving all the time."

Little comfort for Tina! They talked for a couple of minutes and Tina got up to leave.

"Do I see you after the MRI?" she asked

"No. I'll see you on Monday morning when I get the results," the doctor replied.

Tina went out to reception to pay and book an appointment for Monday. While she was waiting, she realised she was looking at a familiar face.

"Hello, Catie," she said. "Long time no see."

Tina had a lot of time for Catie Lanyon. She had been a journalist on many of Tina's big cases. Catie had always rung her before she released any controversial news. It did not always stop her when Tina requested her not to release, but she had at least notified them. More importantly, she was always on the money, and it's hard to argue with that.

"Hi, Inspector. This is not your usual office," replied Catie.

"No, thank goodness," said Tina as Catie walked past on the way to see Dr. Emslie.

"See you later."

"Okay."

Tina drove out of the San and back towards Chatswood. She wondered what this could do to her current case, or her career—or, even worse, her life. She made herself a strong black coffee and headed towards her office.

"Boss, we've been trying to call you. Have you seen today's paper?" It was Detective Broadfinger.

"Sorry Mike. I've had my phone off. No, I haven't seen any of today's news yet. What's up?"

"Our rat has done it again, but this time it's all bullshit," said Mike.

Tina read the headline. 'Riley Sampson—positive lead.' The article went on to say the Delta Taskforce were closing in and the suspect was a northern suburbs furniture removalist with a paedophile history.

Tina breathed deeply "Mike, get Jim Heggarty in here now and stay with me.

Puzzled, Mike went out to get the detective and returned in a few minutes with a very sheepish looking Jim Heggarty. He could not look Tina in the eye.

"Have you seen this, Jim?" Tina threw the paper at him "You should have—you wrote it."

Heggarty baulked. He could hear the threat in her voice "I've no idea what you are talking about."

Mike also looked puzzled.

Tina explained. "Following our meeting on Tuesday I called in a few of the team and told each one a different completely made-up story that they were to tell absolutely no one. I told this one to you only. No one else. How did it end up here, Heggarty?"

"I've no idea. Certainly not me," whined the detective.

"Then you better tell me who you told! You are going to get only one chance to clear this up and that's right now. Let me ask you just once—to save your neck—who did you tell?"

The detective squirmed in his seat looking at the floor. He was clearly uncomfortable. "I was ordered by Detective Sgt. Waldron to keep him up to date with everything I know about the Sampson case."

"Pat Waldron? But he is not stationed here. He has nothing to do with you. Jim—you'd better tell me what's going on *now*. I will offer a peace pipe in return for the full story. If I choose, I can keep you out of it. I am your only chance."

Tina was livid. Waldron was a crooked cop and she had turned him in. She was devastated when he received a minor demotion and a slap on the wrist. He had then threatened her when they were alone.

Heggarty talked. He wanted desperately to stay in the force. He said he had been in cahoots with Pat Waldron and his mates for a few years, in a small way. He outlined their modus operandi, the SP bookies and the brothel owners.

"Jim, this conversation never took place. Leave now and keep going with your work. I don't have to tell you where you will end up if those people find out what you've told us."

Heggarty slunk out of the chief inspector's office. He was mentally exhausted, and worried.

"Holy shit!" Mike exploded. "What are you going to do?"

"Mike, I've got a lot of time for you, and I realise what this means. It's going to be a long road with lots of dangerous corners. I won't play down the risks. I will completely understand if you walk out of here right now, never to discuss this again. I will keep you out of it. As for me, I'm going to try to finish the job I started on Pat Waldron and his rotten crew two years ago. I lost round one—but let's see how I go now."

"I'm in," said Detective Broadfinger, "one hundred percent."

"Great news. I need back up I can trust. It won't be easy. I noticed you flinch when Heggarty said Waldron's main mob contact was Shamus Moriarty. Is that because his name came up at the Riley Sampson meeting on Tuesday?"

"Yeah! I will look into it further to see if I can join any dots. Wow! I wasn't expecting this," said Mike as he was leaving.

Tina drained her coffee, closed her eyes and thought *what a day— the worse health news of my life and a great breakthrough with crooked cops and the mobs—and all in the space of three hours.*

She rang her husband. "David, I'm coming home early. I'll bring tea and the wine. We need to talk."

She hung up much quicker than David did. He stared at the phone. He had a feeling his life was about to change... and he was right.

Chapter Seven

Alvaro stiffened involuntarily, almost falling off his seat. People were watching. Every Tuesday afternoon, he volunteered at the Leichhardt Mission where he was their favourite son. And every Tuesday he bought the *City Paper Bogota* from the Norton Street newsagent. He read the Colombian newspaper from cover to cover, sometimes reading long into the night.

He was sipping coffee at the Mission Café and reading the personal columns when he saw it. He suddenly stopped breathing. A small, simple, advertisement: 'Tagar, contact me.' It had to be Olga.

One of the other volunteers quickly asked, "Alvaro. Are you OK? You look like you've just seen a ghost." They were used to him being the jovial one in the crew, and this reaction was out of character.

Alvaro was used to thinking on his feet. He'd been doing it for nearly fifteen years. "I'm okay. I've just remembered something important I promised to do and didn't." he responded and quickly composed himself. Over the years, he had seen snippets of news about Olga and his family in this paper. They were still fighting the mobs. As far as he could see, Olga had never remarried and was still a Sarmiento."

He once saw a picture of his children, Rodriguez and Zarla, at the Carnivale del Diablo in Rio Sucio. They were with their mother, and growing up fast. It broke his heart. That was a couple of years ago.

He closed his eyes briefly and imagined the luxury of a family hug. Separation was killing him. *There must be a way*, he thought. Particularly as he had now collected a valuable dossier on the mob's Australian operation and all their contacts through listening to his broadening network of close friends.

"How can I contact Olga?" he thought furiously. He knew that if he blew his cover, he would probably be dead within hours. He had seen it happen to others. The mob had some senior contacts both in police and political circles… particularly in Immigration.

That night, Alvaro didn't sleep a wink. He tossed and turned thinking of a hundred ways he might be able to get a message to Olga without giving his identity away. Each one seemed to be fraught with danger either to him, or worse, to Olga and the children.

He reread the tiny advert for the twentieth time 'Tagar, contact me.' He toyed with his breakfast and ate slowly. By mid morning, he had made up his mind. It was now or never. Alvaro could not live the rest of his life doing nothing. He had to take a chance somewhere. Today was the day. He quickly felt better and started to think of a plan. It would have to depend on others, but he was confident he had the right people.

Arriving for work at the markets, he waited till Nick was alone and wandered over. "Boss, I need some advice. Is there anywhere we can talk later?"

Nick 'the Greek' Pashilidis was one person Alvaro would happily trust with his story. Nick was aware Alvaro had never asked for help in his nearly six years of valuable service to his team. "Sure mate. At our dinner break we will head over to the tavern and grab a quiet table. My shout."

Even though he had complete faith in Nick, Alvaro was still very nervous when they ordered and then sat down in a corner. "You once told me I was hiding something. You were right. I am living with a borrowed name. My family and I have been fighting the Colombian Drug Cartels and organised crime for many years and I need to contact my family with valuable information."

"I want to get word through to my wife and children without giving myself away or putting them in danger," Alvaro blurted out. "I don't know where to start." He was outside his comfort zone.

Alvaro could see Nick's mind ticking over. He was taking his time. Alvaro suddenly thought he may have made the wrong move.

"Alvaro, you are right. I know the mobs are active throughout the markets and are closely connected to the Feds. They murder whistle blowers at will. What I can offer is this. A few years ago, some market mobsters and their crooked cops were exposed. We were very thankful. That was a rare thing. I was able to help the investigators at the time and did get to know the top cop who ran the whole operation very well; a trusted, honest, and clever crime fighter. We are still in touch on rare occasions."

"I will make contact and set up a meeting. Not here at the markets and, from what you are telling me, not at the police station where they have facial recognition cameras. You have my personal guarantee you will be in safe, trustworthy and capable hands. After that, it is up to you. I don't need to know anything, but I can probably add to your information."

Over dinner, he gave Alvaro some crucial intelligence that allowed him to connect up other areas of his dossier. They talked and ate, then went back to work at the stall.

Just before knockoff, Nick came over to Alvaro and handed him a slip of paper. "The Chief Inspector is happy to talk to you. She is prepared to listen and advise but no guarantees. Two things: One, she is good and two, she is completely trustworthy."

Alvaro looked at the slip of paper with Tina's name and private mobile number. He breathed deeply. "This is it," Alvaro said out loud. "Thanks Nick." He shook Nicks hand aggressively.

Driving home Alvaro was smiling. He felt that finally something good was about to happen.

Chapter Eight

Catie Lanyon was out of sorts. What a morning! She sat in the San Hospital coffee shop sipping a frothy latte and thought it through—her normal practice when facing serious challenges.

Seeing Tina Samuels in the doctor's surgery was unexpected. She had dealt with the Detective Chief Inspector on a number of her major stories. She liked and respected her. She wondered if Tina was facing similar health issues to hers.

Catie's appointment with Dr. Emslie went as expected. She was sent to radiology for a mammogram and ultrasound and two hours later sat again with the doctor whom she had known and liked for years.

"Catie these lumps don't look good. I am going to need a biopsy and await the results." Dr. Emslie then proceeded to lay out a number of possibilities—none of them appealing to Catie.

Driving back to the city and to the sports club to meet her boss, Senior Editor Bob Millman, things were playing on Catie's mind. She trusted Bob but was fearful where her bombshell would go from here. She showed her membership and went through to the former journalists' bar. She was surprised to see Bob was not alone. He was sitting with a legend of the media industry—old Herbie Brown.

"G'Day, Catie. Grab a seat. What are you drinking?" Bob asked.

"Just a squash thanks—long day ahead." Catie sank into one of the plush lounge chairs. The club name may have changed, but this was still one of their favourite haunts.

Bob came back with the drinks. "Catie I've known you a long time and sense that you are on to something too big to handle on your own. In my forty-five years at the desk, and through many huge stories, I have only ever trusted one man totally, so I have asked Herb to join us, and I hope you trust my judgement."

Catie thought quickly. She did trust Bob and his judgement. She had only heard great things about the tough old bull—Herb.

Over the next hour they discussed many issues, including Catie's current criminal gang bombshell. No mention was made of Catie's health challenges, and she was careful not to name her sources. Catie just told them that she was one hundred percent sure of the details. She was pleased to see the reaction of both the men.

"Wow. This is huge," Bob Millman said as Herb nodded. "You'll need to protect your source."

Herb's first suggestion made Catie realise the dangers involved. "First, these complete details are to be written out and placed in three safe places before you proceed. It's insurance in case anything happens to you. Next, we need to come up with a senior police contact who you trust implicitly, and there are a number of gooduns. The final thing would be to part-involve two influential politicians—one from each side and, again, there are some good choices. If there is one thing I know in all of these cases, the really good folk want the bad eggs out," Herb rasped. "But tread carefully. One wrong choice could put you in mortal danger. This is bigger than the Fitzgerald Inquiry, and these people are not going to take it lying down."

Bob offered his full support and suggested they all go away and reconvene on Friday. Catie agreed but said she had other appointments looming and needed to confirm her available times tomorrow.

Bob then said, "Meantime, Catie, I need you to follow up on another baffling story that's breaking. It may keep your mind off this for a while, and that may keep you safe."

Bob then outlined the story of a returned soldier, Brad Spruce—a hero who had fallen on tough times. Bob was convinced this highly decorated SAS sergeant was a top man, but there were suggestions that all was not as it seemed and reports were coming through that the War Crimes Commission were looking into several allegations about Brad's unit.

"I know Brad well and he will see you if you mention my name. You can take it from there in any direction you feel is right."

They left the club and Catie decided to strike while the iron was hot. She rang Brad. Once she dropped Bob Millman's name, Brad immediately said, "If Bob sent you, I am happy to see you at any time."

They agreed on the next day at ten a.m., at his home. Catie then drove home to work on her own computer. She spent an hour or so typing/changing until she was happy. She then printed off four copies.

Catie was nervous. This was the biggest challenge she had ever faced. Not for the first time, she feared for her life, but she was determined to see it through.

CHAPTER NINE

Brad

Catie was in new territory. She was not familiar with the north west and the Hills district and was pleasantly surprised at the beautiful dwellings and neat, tree-lined streets of Glenhaven. She pulled up in front of a stylish two-storey brick home with, well-maintained, colourful gardens and rang the bell. A very pleasant thirtyish brunette answered the door. "Hi—I'm Catie Lanyon from World News Inc. I've..."

"Hello Catie. Come on in. I'm Jane Spruce. Brad is waiting in the back garden. Tea or coffee?" She smiled.

"Tea thanks—black, no sugar."

Over the next two hours, Catie really warmed to this amazing couple. They talked in circles about many things... life, the commandos, Afghanistan, P.T.S.D. the Hills district and more. Jane told Catie about Brad's Victoria Cross award and his reluctance to say much about it.

Brad was built like the proverbial brick outhouse, and very fit. He was really struggling with his P.T.S.D., the downers, the mood swings, and the toll it was taking on their relationship. He had tried lots of things and had been in some dark places.

He had spent a lot of time with the terrific team at Soldier On, in Concord, and took a great deal on board. He wished Mates 4 Mates would start up in Sydney. He had a close colleague in Brisbane whom he saw often—Bert Hunter—a keen surfboat rower who had similar challenges but seemed to be doing well.

Brad was open on any area Catie probed. He was more reticent when talking about his own exploits. Asked about the day he earned the Victoria Cross, he was quick to point out it was a whole of team effort and he was the one who had received all the accolades. On the potential of war crimes in his unit he was very open.

"It was a dangerous, unpredictable war zone. Not everything

went to plan and there were a few—not many—who let us down. Hindsight is an easy word and I am sure with hindsight we could have done better. But I can truly say, my command were a top bunch and did little to be ashamed of. I am proud of our behaviour and achievements and it hurt to hear these innuendos—most from people who weren't there."

Catie believed him.

Brad also gave Catie the contact details of a number of his team in Sydney, Brisbane and Tasmania, in case she wanted more information.

Catie left just after noon, promising to return in the near future, after she had looked into the whole story. She felt she was capable of turning it into a good feature.

Jane and Brad were genuinely warm in their invitation for Catie to come back at any time. She knew she would be welcome and thought that if ever she was in a tight battle situation that Brad would be a great person to have at her side. Later events would prove just how accurate that was.

Catie drove out of the leafy Hills District and back to the city via her bank and her solicitor's office, dropping off sealed envelopes at both. Back at the office she thought long and hard about Herb Brown's suggestions.

Maybe yesterday was an omen. She picked up the phone and dialled the direct number of Detective Chief Inspector Tina Samuels. Catie had made up her mind.

Chapter Ten

Winter had well and truly settled in. The chilly mornings had seen frost on the leaf-covered ground in Epping, but things were warming up behind the scenes at work. The past month had been frantic on so many fronts.

As if Tina didn't have enough on her plate, she had fielded two phone calls in three days that had ignited all her good police instincts, and she could never resist a challenge. *But why now?*

The first call was from Catie Lanyon, two days after she had run into her at Dr. Emslie's surgery. Tina had great respect for Catie's ethics and abilities and thought she sounded worried. She readily agreed to meet her and both of them realised they had appointments at the San Hospital in two day's time. So, with a little juggling, a time was organised. A good neutral venue: the hospital coffee shop.

The second call came from a man she saw little of. Nick Pashilidis was a great guy. He was Greek and a respected and well-liked manager of one of the fruit and veggie businesses at the Sydney markets. Nick had been instrumental in getting Tina the evidence she needed to expose Detective Pat Waldron and his crooked mates. She owed him.

Nick was really concerned for one of his long-time staff of whom he thought the world. He gave Tina a brief background on Alvaro and his situation. It sounded ominous, and she thought she may be able to offer some assistance and advice, but no guarantees.

Tina told Nick to have him ring her on her silent number.

Tina's health news had been shattering. Dr Emslie had confirmed lung cancer—early onset. He prescribed eight weeks of chemotherapy at the San Cancer Clinic. David had proved to be a great shoulder to lean on and immediately offered to down tools and do whatever was needed. She was not looking forward to Friday's appointment with the medico.

Tina's meeting with Catie at the hospital coffee shop was far more intriguing than she thought. For a few minutes, they compared current health news and the irony of them both knowing Dr Marie Emslie so well and for so long. Then, they got onto the subject of Catie's grave concern.

Catie quickly realised she had made the right call in ringing Tina. She spent nearly an hour giving her every single detail of the mob members, the protectors, the many areas of operations, drugs distribution, SP bookmaking, race fixing, brothels, plus intimate details of the recent gangland murders at Vaucluse—times, places, weapons used and, most importantly, where the murder weapons had been disposed.

Tina's eyes rolled when Waldron's name came out as Moriarty's protector and informant on impending raids and various investigations. Then again, when Jim Heggarty was mentioned as 'Waldron's bagman'. She was angry, having realised Heggarty had only given her a tiny bit of his dealings with Waldron and Co.

At the end of their fact finding session, Catie gave Tina a sealed envelope. She looked around the coffee shop, but no one appeared to be taking any notice of them.

"Catie, the good news is, I have a senior straight cop who can put together a strike force and, with all this, we can build a watertight case. It will be dangerous. You need to go to ground. Say nothing to anyone else and we will continue to work on what news is to be released and when. Tell Anita to lie low, but keep an eye on her and make sure we keep her safe. We will need her help. Give her an emergency code signal and your mobile phone number. Maybe give her mine too as a backup."

One half of Tina was excited, the other worried. This was big.

Catie took it all in. She had already been advised she was going to need a radiation treatment course. She thought she could escape Sydney and head north, to her mum's on the Gold Coast, for treatment there. She could still work on her computer yet stay hidden.

The following Monday, Tina's phone buzzed with no caller ID. It was Alvaro. She thought he spoke good English and agreed to meet him the next day, Tuesday, at a charity coffee shop in Norton Street Leichhardt.

Alvaro was sitting alone reading his Colombian paper as he said he would, so she picked him straight away. She was not expecting such a monumental brief.

Tina liked Alvaro from the start. He was a handsome man, had a genuine manner, kind eyes and strong voice. He was obviously intelligent. Nick had been spot on.

Alvaro, on the other hand, was not comfortable risking everything with a total stranger. After some general discussion, and Tina telling Alvaro how Nick had been invaluable in their successful efforts to trap crooked cops, he relaxed and decided *this is it—boots and all. Take the risk,* he thought to himself.

Alvaro then told Tina the full story, from Bogata through Indonesia and then his Australian journey. "My real name is Bernardo Rodriguez Sarmiento," he began and then detailed his full story.

Tina was absorbed with his tale. She wondered, *how can one person put up with so much over such a long period.* She realised she was talking with a true survivor in every sense of the word; obviously a good man who wanted to right many wrongs.

Tina breathed in sharply when Alvaro named Carlos Carezo as the market's cartel organiser, and his cohort, Shamus Moriarty, the king-pin of the organised crime gang. She wondered just how far this venomous web can stretch.

Alvaro saw her flinch and asked, "Do you know these men?" Tina replied that yes, she did, and that they had formed part of another investigation she was involved in. After hearing him out, Tina said straight up

"Alvaro—we will continue with that name for the time being— when Nick called me, I was prepared to see you as a favour to him and give whatever advice I could. I now realise how important it is for you to get a message through to Olga without any risk to her. I think I can make that happen safely."

Alvaro's eyes lit up.

"And, I also realise how much of your story correlates to our other investigations and your new information fits squarely with our findings.

I am currently working with a trusted investigative journalist whose life is in danger from these criminals, just as yours is. I have told her—and I now tell you—I have a trustworthy and well connected senior police executive in my corner. I will sit with him and then come back to you both with a way forward. I really hope this is the start of a very positive era in your life's story. I think it will be."

They were just winding up when a fellow suddenly stopped next to them. "Alvaro, my friend, what brings you here?" he said in a high-pitched voice. It was one of the office staff from the markets.

"I volunteer here every Tuesday—for the mission," Alvaro explained. "I am about to start now."

"Good people," said the fellow and walked off. Tina watched him go. She had seen him somewhere before.

Both Tina and Alvaro left the mission coffee shop and went their respective ways, both feeling it had been a really good move to get together. Tina sat in her car and tried to make sense of everything that came out of the past couple of weeks. She dialled the police Commissioner direct—something she had never done before.

"Palmer," answered an authoritative voice

"Commissioner, this is Chief Inspector Samuels. I need to see you in private and as soon as possible."

"Well, Tina, given that you have never called me before, I can only imagine it is important. You name a time and a place and I'll be there."

She gave the commissioner a time and place, then drove home to bring David up to speed.

Chapter Eleven

Garth and Meg Peterson were enjoying the twilight, sipping a wine on the open back porch of their magnificent canal front second home, reflecting about life. The weekend sun was casting a beautiful orange glow above the clouds as it set behind the Tamborine Mountains.

Meg was concerned that Garth was internalising all his misgivings since his bladder cancer diagnoses. He had always been like that, a stoical person to a fault. She knew he was worried about next Tuesday's cystoscopy surgery at Pindara Private Hospital but could see no way she could improve things.

She was right, Garth's thoughts were all over the place, unusual for him. He was used to challenges, but never with his own health. Usually he was dealing with things he knew a lot about and he was in control. But this was different.

'Dr Google' was not helping. There were so many negative possibilities.

He was reflecting, thinking about life after the Wheat Corporation. He was well aware that his meteoric rise through the ranks at CRC had brought him to the top of the corporate ladder. Life had treated them well over the years. Offers had come in thick and fast, and he had moved with them as appropriate. Many of his achievements were successful and rewarding.

He smiled to himself over the demise of Bob Leeson as Chairman of the Board a few years after he left. Garth had been brooding over his Wheat Board misgivings since joining CRC. One day, he met a clever journalist who had previously uncovered some major faults in the Australian transport industry and brought it to heel. He had a lot of respect for young Catie Lanyon and had gotten to know her well. She was thorough and had a nose for finding malpractices and exposing them. One day, at an industry convention, he had opened up to Catie about his time at the Wheat Board and his disquiet at the realisation that nothing had changed. That's all it took. Catie started to sniff around and then things escalated, as media questions went from a small story on page nineteen to front-page headlines in just a few weeks.

Bob Leeson fell on his sword. Underhand payments to third parties, massive unreported losses in grain stock and special arrangements between Leeson and five of the silo owners all came to light. All bad news for Leeson.

Garth knew that things at the Wheat Board had improved markedly since his friend, Rob Champion, was appointed chairman. He was pleased about that, and that Rob had appointed Evelyn Goldsmith as CEO. They never looked back.

He smiled when he thought of Rob. A couple of years ago, one of Garth's 'Babbling Brook' stud yearlings had won the Randall Champion Memorial Handicap at the Gold Coast Turf Club meeting. Garth was surprised when Randall's son, Rob, presented him with the trophy. It was a genuinely warm handshake with both of them laughing, "What a small world."

Over a beer in the members' bar afterwards, Rob ventured, "I've been watching your success in the big wide world. Well done. I have often wondered if you had anything to do with the public upheaval at the Wheat Board Corporation."

"It could be said I threw the first snowball, but it was tiny. The roll on even took me by surprise."

"Well, thanks. You did Australia a great service."

They talked on into the afternoon.

Garth had since gone on to be Chairman of the Board in a number of successful major corporations and organisations. He had every reason to be happy with his lot. That is until now. Dr. Chas Chaperonne was a first-class urologist and surgeon. Garth had been well referred. Tests discovered that the cancer had penetrated three layers of muscle and tissue but was still contained inside the bladder.

"This is very encouraging, and our success with treating early diagnosed cancers is good news for you," the doctor told Garth. "We will know more after Tuesday."

Garth had many questions, but felt it a bit early to ask. He would wait until after next week's cystoscopy.

The following Tuesday, Garth was early to register at Pindara reception. He had been fasting since eight p.m. last evening, when the anaesthetist had phoned. He sent Meg on her way. The hospital advised they would call her later in the day, when he was wheeled into the recovery ward. Meg was nervous, but left. There was nothing she could do here.

After registering him and filling out all the paperwork, a volunteer took Garth down to day surgery, where he was processed by the Triage sister. He sat with the other patients in a hallway to await his turn. There were no frills here. He had a nervous pee in the adjacent toilet and then waited for over an hour.

"Mr Peterson," called the nurse. Garth jumped up nervously. He would get used to it later. He was ushered into cubical six and told to put on the surgical gown. Ugly!

I'll bet none of these have ever been stolen, he thought to himself. *These have never been seen on a catwalk in a fashion parade.*

Next, the transport orderly wheeled him through many corridors at great speed, pressing green buttons that made doors magically open for them.

Garth remembered chatting to the anaesthetist, Olive, as she steered the needle into his veins, and that was it. A couple of hours later, he woke in the recovery ward. He had a catheter coming out of his penis. It was full of red liquid. He looked up to see two bags hanging on the side of the bed. Saline solutions were dripping into his veins from above.

The recovery nurse was pleasant. "Dr. Chaperonne will see you soon," she chirped, "and your wife is waiting patiently in the lounge."

When the doctor arrived, he advised Garth, "All went well. I have taken several specimens for biopsy. I'm afraid you will be with us overnight and we'll see if the line is clear and you pass the pee test tomorrow. You may need to carry the bag for a week or so."

Meg was waiting as he was transferred into the ward.

A week later, Garth was back in hospital for the removal of the bag. It had been a tough seven days. After the confirmation of the cancer, he had long discussions about his options with his urologist and oncologists.

Garth and Meg decided on a two-month radiation course, daily Monday to Friday, at a Southport cancer clinic. Two days before he was due to start, he came home from the surgery with a wry smile and said to Meg, "Guess what. I've just got three tattoos."

Meg nearly fainted until Garth explained they were the radiation markers. Tiny Xs.

The big day arrived and Garth presented himself at the radiation clinic. After completing the obligatory paper-work, he was directed to a seat to await his call. There were about half a dozen waiting, mainly women. He sat down next to a young lady in a light blue scarf.

"Well, hello Garth" she said brightly.

Garth had to look twice to recognise Catie Lanyon.

"Goodness me, Catie," he smiled. "Meg and I were only talking about you last week. Long time no see," he said. They briefly compared health stories until Catie was called for treatment.

Chapter Twelve

Tina was a few minutes early at Circular Quay. She purchased two full-day ferry excursion tickets and sat under the terminal indicator board looking out over the harbour towards Luna Park. She was in a no-nonsense mood. Her early morning meeting with Jim Heggarty was sobering. When she fronted him with Waldron's 'bag man' evidence, he had flinched. Tina stood her ground... and there were no niceties.

She gave him two options. The first was to resign immediately, tell *everything* he knew, and then go into witness protection. The second was that Tina would put the word out that he had already agreed to 'sing'. Both of them knew he would be dead within hours if that got out.

Heggarty was shattered.

Tina softened a little. "Jim, there can be many valid reasons how and why it has come to this. I am prepared to go to bat for you if you work fully with me. Every one of us has done something we are not proud of and every one of us gets a chance to redeem themselves at some point, and put things straight. This is your one and only chance."

Heggarty needed no convincing. He couldn't work out how it had come to this. He knew Tina was a no nonsense, straight shooter. It was his only option. He sang— this time, long and loud.

Tina had called in Mike Broadfinger. The full interview was filmed and recorded. It was explosive evidence and curtains for Waldron and others. "I'll have my resignation, guns and ID on your desk in ten minutes," he said flatly. "I'll just need to clean out my desk."

"Sorry, Jim," said Tina. "You've passed that point. You will resign here and now and hand in your goods and chattels, including your phone. I need to go through your desk myself."

Heggarty slumped forward in the seat, totally defeated. He knew Tina was right. There were things he did not want her to find. But he wanted to live. He gave in.

Detective Broadfinger quietly instigated a safe house with no one else involved. He handcuffed Heggarty, covered the cuffs with a jacket and left the office with him.

When Tina had finished going through Heggarty's desk, and after organising a search of his home, it was time to leave and meet the commissioner.

Commissioner Palmer strolled onto pier three, complete with sports shirt, snappy hat, man-bag and sunglasses. He looked as if he was heading for Manly and a day on the beach.

They grabbed takeaway coffee and boarded the off-peak ferry. There were plenty of quiet spots at this time of the day. They picked an open area on the top deck and settled in for the return crossing.

Tina hardly drew breath for the entire outward journey. She began with Catie's involvement and Anita's revelations, leaving nothing out. She then detailed the initial trap set for Jim Heggarty, through to his signed confession details, arrest and transfer to the safe house this morning. She then told the remarkable story of Alvaro's fourteen year journey from Colombia, right through to the Sydney markets, and all his research and organised crime details. It was a huge brief.

"So, Commissioner, these have all come together. We now have all the witnesses and information we need to intercept this massive drug shipment, blow the mobs wide open, and get full convictions. All we need to do is keep the four witnesses alive."

It took the commissioner a few minutes to marshal his thoughts. Tina was in no hurry. She knew the bombshell she had dropped. By this time, they had reached Manly. The amusement pier was busy and people were enjoying the huge protected swimming pool near the Aquarium. The ferry began re-boarding. Tina went off to refill their coffee and felt the throbbing of those big motors starting to increase revolutions as she returned to the deck, just as they were pulling out from the wharf. They took little notice of a pod of dolphins that appeared to be escorting them towards the heads.

John Palmer opened up. "Tina. I have been in the force for forty-one years. From day one and my probationary training at Goulburn, I have dreamt of something this big. It always seemed like 'only in

Hollywood'. This is an enormous challenge and will have major judicial, political and gangland ramifications worldwide if we pull it off. Or a lot of funerals, including our own, if we fail," he said quietly. "You have done an amazing job to get this far and collate so much irrefutable evidence and credible witnesses. We owe it to the rest of the world and our Oath of Office to give it our best shot. Truthfully, I am a little afraid, but super excited. I believe we can do it. I cannot thank you enough."

"This is my plan," he went on. "You go back to Chatswood and the Riley Sampson case. We will play down Heggarty's sudden departure with an ill-health concocted story to defuse the situation there. But it will send out signals.

"I have a few key contacts I can completely trust, one of them may surprise you. You need to give my judgement your full blessing. We will make this a small task force with no admin support, but the power to co-opt where necessary. We need total secrecy and only yourself and Mike Broadfinger will be in the loop from your end. You need to hand pick a backup team for the intercept, but no info to them yet."

The commissioner went on to advise that Alvaro should keep that name for the moment. Tina's immediate responsibility was to keep Catie and Alvaro isolated and to protect Anita as well as possible, with no support staff. With Heggarty, he suggested only handpicked troops be rostered to do security at his safe house.

"I will get you enough cash to achieve whatever needs to be done. I will set up a strike team ready to go anywhere for anything we set up. As soon as I put the wheels in motion, we will have our next meeting," the commissioner concluded.

"Thanks, Sir. Sounds good to me. By the way, there are some more developments on the Riley Sampson case. I will get them to you in the next day or so."

"Tina, please call me John. We are to get into complicated territory soon and first names are easier and safer."

"No worries, Sir" replied Tina. She was going to find that hard.

The ferry pulled into Circular Quay and the commissioner disembarked. Tina stayed on board. She would take a taxi from Manly Wharf to the office. Meantime she had some important phone calls to make and meetings to set up. She was thinking they were going to need that cash. She was taking no notice of the gently rolling swell and small sailing craft as they cruised back to Manly under a blazing sun.

Chapter Thirteen

Tina was trying to stay calm. Over the past few days, she was thrown back into the Riley Sampson case with real energy. One line was progressing. Detective McHenry had unearthed that Riley's dad, Real Estate Agent Rick Sampson, was a heavy gambler on the gallopers. Georgia had called in to check on Riley's mum, Jan. They were becoming close and Georgia decided to ask some personal questions.

"So what caused you and Rick to split?"

"Slow horses," Jan had replied immediately. "Rick loves the races but has little success. He borrowed forty thousand dollars from my dad. Told him it was to invest in a block of land at Kellyville, but it turned out it was to pay his SP bookmaker."

"Did your dad get it all back?" asked Georgia.

"Not a cent. It broke my heart and I left. That was the last straw."

"Was he ever violent or aggressive?" Georgia asked.

"Not really. He gets depressed when he loses. Most people like him a lot. He seems to do well at work."

"How is your relationship now? Does he visit Riley?"

"That's the problem. He loves Riley and is has visitation rights every two weeks. But he is way behind in maintenance and we are back in the family court at the moment. It makes life hard. My parents despise him and he knows it."

Georgia had, after this, quietly canvassed the area around his agency at West Pennant Hills. She learnt that Rick was popular, but she also picked up that he had seemed nervous and moody over the past month or so. His associates put it down to Riley's disappearance. They all knew he idolised his son.

Georgia went to see Rick at his shop late one morning. She immediately picked up on his unease.

"How come you are getting nowhere?" he demanded. "You people are supposed to be good at this." His anger showed.

"Well, Mr Sampson, we have followed many leads and gone over them time and again. There is something strange here. No sign of any struggle, no ransom demand and no evidence that he has fallen victim to foul play. This is highly unusual. We keep running into brick walls," said the detective. "But someone, somewhere, knows exactly what is happening. All we need is to know who. By the way, Mr Sampson, I understand you like to punt on the horses. Can I be so bold as to ask if that is a profitable exercise?"

Clearly, Rick was not expecting this, and he almost sat bolt upright. "My private life has nothing to do with this mess. For your information it is only a hobby," he blurted. Georgia thought, *your father-in-law may dispute that*, but said nothing.

"If I were you, I would look closely at all the peddos who live near Narrabeen," Rick wheezed loudly, "and stop wasting valuable time on me." He was starting to sweat.

Georgia was convinced she had hit a nerve. All was not as it seemed here. After a few more probes the detective left Rick's office. On a hunch, she rang Detective Henderson from her car. "Brad, I need a favour. I need someone to stake out Rick Sampson's real estate office at Thompsons Corner, and we need to get a bug into his office. Can you help?"

"Yeah, sure Georgia, I reckon a couple of would-be clients could leave a device somewhere. I'll start with some phone monitoring just for insurance. How long do you need the stakeout?"

"Great, thanks Bradley. After this morning's meeting something could happen very soon. So, just office hours until Friday... no, make that Saturday—race day."

"Will do. Anything else I need to know?"

Georgia gave Brad a rundown of her meetings with both Sue and Rick, and his unease. She also said that a few close to him had seen a distinct mood change recently. Georgia thought she had better bring the chief inspector up to date and rang Tina's mobile.

"Hi Georgia, what's new?" said Tina, seeing the detectives name on the screen.

"A few things, Chief. First, I need to bring you up to date with my latest meetings with Riley's mother and father and a few of his father's associates. Secondly, as a result, I have asked Brad Henderson to set up a surveillance of the real estate agency and to plant a listening device."

"Okay. Are you coming in this arvo?"

"I'll be there in half an hour. I just need to grab a snack downstairs," Georgia replied.

"Great. I'll be out for an hour or so. See you as soon as I get back." Tina hung up. She called Mike Broadfinger into the office. "Don't sit down. Grab pen and paper. We're going for a drive."

They grabbed take away coffee in The Cell coffee shop in the foyer, then went to the basement and drove down Fullers Road. They found a bench in the shade at Blue Gum Reserve in the Lane Cove National Park and began to talk.

"This should do the trick. Let me start by telling you that when all the pieces of this jigsaw puzzle are in place, the effects will be seen and heard around the world. Let's see if we can put it together. No easy task." Tina said. "You listen. I'll talk. Then I'll take any questions you like."

For some thirty minutes, between sips, Tina updated Mike on the Riley case, then quickly got on to her meeting with Commissioner Palmer. She itemised everything she could remember in as close to chronological order as she could. When she finally drew breath, Mike just uttered one word: "wow". He was stuck for anything else to say.

"Here's how it needs to go from here. You'd better add these to your notes. First, we have to make sure there are no bugs in either of our offices. You'll need to make it look like a standard whole of office check so no one is alarmed. If, at any time, this starts to get messy, we need to cover all our bases. Next, add a few new CTV cameras in appropriate places for our two offices and have them monitored daily for the night before. Any blackouts need to be reported.

"Our own meetings should be outside where possible, and certainly after the strike force meets. By the way, the commissioner has given us a new name 'Strike Force Cleanout'."

"Very appropriate," Mike commented.

Tina went on. "As a matter of urgency, we need to get Alvaro and Catie underground and into safe places. Plus, Catie needs to warn Anita that things are about to warm up and to be very observant. Leave that to me. We need to give Anita an escape route. Then we need to get a small back-up team of our own trusted people to be ready to galvanise into action at a minute's notice, and it could be dangerous. We need, say, six. They will report to you. Any suggestions?"

"Well, certainly Georgia and Brian Carey from Delta, and we could name two each from outside missing persons."

"Okay," said Tina. "When we get them together, away from the missing persons office, I suggest we give them a general briefing but no names or vital specifics yet. We need to convince them of the international magnitude of this case without revealing too much, just in case. But they must be ready to drop everything on a moment's notice and respond to whatever emergency arises."

Tina went on to tell Mike that Commissioner Palmer was putting the Taskforce together ASAP. "All I know, at this point, is that it will be small. He and I, plus three outsiders in key roles both in Australia and overseas, We have no option but to trust his judgement—and I do," she concluded.

As they were heading back Tina said, "And Mike, I need to tell you I have a few serious health issues at the moment and will be spending disproportionate time on various treatments. I will keep you in the loop, but no one else needs to know."

Mike gently said, "Whatever it is Chief, I can cover for you. Just let me know what you want, and good luck."

Georgia was waiting when they got back. She expanded on the Riley Sampson developments, both her own news and a few other leads coming in from the rest of the team, including a couple of new leads from Narrabeen itself. She also invited Tina to her hen's night in three weeks' time. Tina smiled and accepted, then suggested another team update briefing for Friday morning. She felt things might be on the improve if only they could link all the clues. She then asked Georgia for a roster of those on the Thompsons Corner surveillance and to be kept up to date. She also told Georgia, she would soon be working on another case alongside Mike and herself.

"Say nothing," she warned.

Something was nagging at Tina. Just on a hunch, she went to the file room and extracted her notes from the earlier police corruption case. She wondered what Waldron was up to. As she flipped through the pages, Tina suddenly froze. A mug shot. She hadn't remembered him. It was one of Waldron's informants from the markets, David Gillespie. He was the same guy who spoke to Alvaro at the Leichhardt Café.

Tina went cold. She called Alvaro's mobile. He answered quickly. "Where are you?" she asked.

"At the markets. I've just started the afternoon shift. Is something wrong?"

"Could be, Alvaro. I want you to go to Nick *now*. Tell him you are not well and need to see a doctor. Catch a taxi to the nearest medical centre and walk in. After the taxi goes, walk back out, then walk one or two blocks and catch a second taxi home. I will be there. Do it right now Alvaro, and keep your eyes open for anything unusual."

Tina hung up, grabbed Mike and left for Annandale. "Put the siren on but turn it off as we leave the city," ordered Tina. "Here's hoping we're not too late." She then rang a city detective she knew and organised backup to stand by a few blocks away—just in case.

Chapter Fourteen

Tina turned the siren off as they left the city and sped north along Parramatta Road. They turned right into Annandale Road just in time to see a yellow cab driving off and Alvaro heading inside the old style, dark brick tenement building.

"So far, so good," sighed Tina as they pulled up outside 98. "Let's go in—Unit 3."

Alvaro was already packing. He didn't have much. Tina told him to take few clothes and anything he did not want others to find. "We've got one minute, Alvaro," barked Tina, and then told him that she had recognised Dave Gillespie as one of the mob's contacts from her previous dealings with corruption.

"I'm sure he would have recognised my face," she puffed as they literally raced down the hallway towards the street carrying bags. "I'm also sure he would have told Carezo."

About half an hour before this, Nick Pashalidis had been concerned when Alvaro said he was not well. He looked very scared. He also noted that one of the labourers on the stall opposite had seen Alvaro go and had hurried down to the market's admin office. Things weren't looking right. He thought he would make a phone call as soon as the next truck left.

Tina, Alvaro and Mike bundled into the unmarked police car just as her phone rang. It was Nick Pashalidis.

"It's okay Nick. We are with Alvaro now and all is well but, I am sorry, Alvaro won't be back until this is over," said Tina, and then told Nick of their Leichhardt meeting and recognising Dave Gillespie.

"Good. I will cover for Alvaro here," said Nick. He then told her about the guy opposite who had run to the office seemingly to report Alvaro's movements. "God be with you," said Nick.

Mike Broadfinger turned the car towards the city just as reports were coming over the police radio calling all cars to a medical centre in Glebe Point Road, where some sort of major ruckus was taking place. Police were nearby and quickly in attendance.

"That's where I went after the markets," Alvaro hissed.

Tina smiled. "Just in time. Let's hope we stay in front. Within minutes they will be in your flat."

Tina brought Alvaro up to speed on a number of fronts. She told him they were forming a new special task force of top operators to combine his intelligence with material from other sources. She predicted things would move fast from here.

Alvaro was really pleased to hear Tina was working on a plan to get a message safely to Olga.

"Do you like fishing?" Tina asked Alvaro

"Yes I do. We used to fish all the time back in Bogata," he reminisced. "Why?"

"Because when you shave off that facial hair and dye the rest blond, you will be living on a Gold Coast canal, in a small unit, and you will do precious little more than eat, sleep, exercise and fish for the next few weeks."

Alvaro was happy to get the car keys of the old Commodore, plus a new licence from Mike Broadfinger. He had already shaved and was feeling different. He had not been clean shaven since he was a boy. His bare skin felt and looked strange.

"Now Alvaro, do not speed or break any traffic laws. This car is registered to Alvaro Samalez and that is the name on your new driver's licence, with no photo. That is also the name we have booked the unit under. The last thing we need is a traffic cop putting all this information into the system. It could get messy."

Alvaro understood. He was amazed when Mike gave him $5,000 in one-hundred-dollar notes.

"Whatever happens, no credit cards, Medicare or the like from now on, just cash. We don't want to see any trace of you. And here is a new phone. Switch the old one off now and leave it with me. You will be contacted by one of our associates. Her name is Catie. She will be around to see you after a couple of days."

Alvaro was pleased with all the attention to detail. He felt safer. He decided to have his hair cut and dyed in a town on the way, so he would arrive as Alvaro Samalez. He was also keen to buy some fishing gear.

Back at the office, Tina rang the commissioner to update him on their escape with Alvaro.

"Tina. We are dealing with the worst scum here. I was just about to call you. Word has just come through. We received word of gunfire at the markets a few minutes ago. Nick Pashalidis' body has just been found. He was apparently lured out the back and butchered. I reckon it will be the mob. I'm sorry Tina. I know he was special to you and a terrific fellow. These bastards are really trying to cover their tracks."

"I'll see you at the meeting tomorrow."

Tina was shattered. Tears welled. She knew she was responsible. She vaguely remembered the commissioner talking about tomorrow's meeting. She needed to be there. Her eyes closed. She could feel tears coming again. Nick, I promise you, *we'll get these bastards*, she pledged to herself.

Chapter Fifteen

Commissioner John Palmer wasted no time in getting a call out to three trusted allies whom he felt needed to involve at this point. Alan McDonald was Deputy Commissioner of the Australian Federal Police and had been John's closest friend, both professionally and socially, for some thirty-five years. Tall and imposing, with a ready smile, his speciality was the new border force set up and the AFP's protective services unit. He lived in Canberra, but spent most weekends at his other home on Circuit Beach, Lilli Pilli, near Batemans Bay. He loved the peace and solitude, the rolling waves below, and rock fishing.

Warren Hardcastle had been one of John's deputy commissioners for the past three years. Hardcastle had joined the NSW Police about twenty-five years ago, when he was seconded as a single man from Scotland Yard in the UK to work with the NSW Police on his speciality—internal investigations. He definitely had the English pink cheeks and a plum in his mouth. Warren never returned to the old dart. He loved Australia, went back to university part-time and married a fellow uni graduate, Tiah Bryson, from Sydney's northern beaches. They now lived at Manly, just above Fairlight, overlooking the magnificent harbour on the pathway down to the kids' favourite rock-pool. They juggled a busy lifestyle with three daughters. Tiah had her own legal practice.

Rusty Nolan was different. A well-known and flamboyant rugby league director, renowned for his ability to get things done, he had been linked, over the years, to a number of questionable characters and situations. But the continuous media questions and innuendos had proved nothing. His mates called him, 'Teflon', as nothing ever sticks to Rusty.

But behind the scenes, John Palmer knew a very different Rusty. They had worked closely and successfully for years, unbeknownst to the rest of the world.

Their meeting was scheduled for ten a.m. at their usual spot in the Eastern Suburbs Rugby Leagues Club plush boardroom. This gave Alan McDonald time to fly in from Canberra and get across. As a director, Rusty Nolan was always at the club, so there were no eyebrows raised. John Palmer and Warren Hardcastle were already club members and regulars. All four men had worked together on a number of successful covert assignments over the years, and chatted away on general matters whilst making a cuppa.

The doors closed after Rusty came in and they sat down.

"Good morning all. This is the one we've been waiting for," the commissioner began, and for the next fifteen minutes he pieced together all the snippets of information they had so far gleaned from Tina, Anita Collins, Alvaro Palez, Catie Lanyon and Jim Heggarty.

"What we know is that there is a massive shipment of drugs leaving Colombia by ship in the next few weeks bound for Sydney. We are fairly sure we have most of what we need regarding the Sydney wharf unloading and Sydney markets distribution channels. Even better, we have a large list of crooked police and border force agents, importers, mob contacts and their political protectors. Between us we can hopefully fill in the gaps and missing links. I have asked Detective Chief Inspector Samuels to join our task force and I've given us a name: 'Operation Cleanout'."

After this, each of the group added what extras they could and each made a list of what they would do next.

Alan McDonald was connected with the Colombian 'good guys', and they discussed the best way of getting Alvaro's message safely to Olga.

Rusty Nolan had a concern. "I know the Moriarty mob well, including Morabito and his girlfriend. 'Wipeout' is a bad piece of shit and she's not much better. I would be very careful what I told her. Loose lips sink ships."

Tina put him at ease. "Worry not. Other than the whole story that she told to the journalist, Anita knows nothing. However, we need her evidence, and we have made plans to put her and her daughter into a safe place if things go pear shaped."

Before they left, the commissioner told all of them that time was of the essence and that he hoped to have more information by Tuesday, so they agreed to meet Wednesday—same time, same place.

"If you can't get me, call Warren. He will be on my right hip for the next couple of months," John Palmer told them. There was an air of excitement as they all went their various ways.

On the way back to Chatswood HQ Tina thought back over the meeting. She had never met Alan MacDonald, but had heard many good reports. She knew Deputy Commissioner Hardcastle and they had always got along extremely well. She loved his English mannerisms, and also got on well with his wife, Tiah, on the many occasions they had met at various functions.

The commissioner had been right. Tina was quite surprised to see Rusty Nolan in the room. She had interviewed him twice before on some heavy matters but had never been able to find anything to take enquiries further. However, the commissioner had asked Tina to 'trust my judgement' and she did.

Chapter Sixteen

Catie was enjoying her new situation in Queensland. Her mother's tastefully decked out townhouse at Clear Island Waters was on a lake's edge, right in the centre of the Gold Coast. Two bedrooms and two bathrooms made it plenty big enough for the two of them. They had daily visits from the swans, dragon lizards and beautiful multicoloured rainbow lorikeets. Their biggest laugh was the cat lady who roamed the complex at all hours, walking her grey furry friend.

She knew her mum was enjoying her company too. It had been almost three years since her dad had passed away and, even though she had a good circle of friends and hobbies, her mum still felt lonely.

Catie's radiation treatment seemed to be going well but was causing her some discomfort and drowsiness, which made her work a bit challenging at times. She had run into Garth four times now. They had enjoyed solving the world's problems while chatting. Garth suggested lunch with Meg and himself 'for old time's sake.'

Catie responded with, "How's about nine a.m. brunch on Thursday? I usually come good by then. I am meeting associates in Brisbane later that afternoon."

Thursday came and they spent a few pleasant hours at the Water's Edge Restaurant on the Isle of Capri, midway between both their homes. Meg confided in Catie that Garth was 'more than happy' when Bob Leeson had been sacked from his chairman's role. They all agreed that the Leesons of this world kept popping up like bad pennies. Meg also lamented that Garth spends way too much time with his horses at 'The Brook', but said it had been very successful. "It keeps him sane," she conceded.

Catie bid them farewell just before noon and headed up the M1 to Brisbane. She always enjoyed a good run in her bright red sports machine. Brad and Jane Spruce were staying with his army buddy, and

Brad wanted Catie to see the Mates 4 Mates complex at Albion, just behind the famous Breakfast Creek Hotel. It was all part of their story.

During the morning, Catie had considered asking Garth's advice on some of her concerns about Anita's and Brad's predicaments, but decided against it for now. She needed to find out a bit more yet. Catie was really worried about Anita's situation. She was in a deadly snake pit and running a huge risk. Catie was pleased when Anita voluntarily reconfirmed her desire to do something good and assist Catie to bring down the mob. She knew that was the right thing to do, and it was her way of getting onto the pathway to salvation, as she saw it.

Catie knew Garth was really well connected at the top of the corporate ladder. She was one hundred percent certain he would be more than happy to 'face up' and root out the bad guys. He had consistently and successfully done that over the years wherever he went.

Anita had originally been a little concerned when Catie had told her she was relocating up north for three months or so for treatment for some health issues, and to stay out of sight. She was happy when they came up with 'Anita now' as the emergency signal to get her out, plus the news that help was only seconds away, 24/7. She was also happy to have Tina's number as a backup. She readily agreed to keep a bag packed, just in case.

"Maybe I could come up to see my Mum," Anita said. "My visit is long overdue. She lives at Mt Gravatt on the Gold Coast side of Brisbane."

They both agreed that would be great if it happened.

Catie eventually found Mates 4 Mates in the side street. She was buzzed into the car park and went into reception. Jane was sipping coffee and reading while Brad was working out in the gym with his mate.

Jane welcomed her. "Hi Catie-Tea, coffee or Bonox?"

"Black tea would be great. No sugar"

They talked for a few minutes before Brad finished his workout and came over. "Hi Catie. I'd like you to meet and old associate of mine, Bert Hunter. Bert, Catie."

They all chatted for a while. Bert gave Catie an inspection and run down on Mates 4 Mates and the good results with the rehabilitation of returned men and women from the various theatres of war.

"P.T.S.D. is a growing curse. It's been around a long while—over one hundred years—but has only recently been recognised and named," said Bert. "The powers-that-be are finally recognising the huge mental issues facing returned personnel. Many great lives have been wasted."

Eventually Brad asked, "So, how is the investigation going? Any luck?"

Catie was a bit hesitant. Brad saw it and said, "It's OK. Bert is completely in the know. He's half of the story."

"Well, the most important thing I have tracked down to date is where all these war crime conspiracy theories are coming from and what, I think, is behind them all. Do the names Boston Ballard or Gerarde Page mean anything to either of you?"

Both boys nodded. "C Battalion," Bert said. "Ballard was an NCO. Very good, hard soldier by all accounts. I worked with him a few times on a couple of tours. Page was in the media corps on the last Afghanistan tour. I think he was a pretty bright journo. Ballard is one of the blokes singled out in some of these stories circulating, but I never saw him in any bad situations."

Brad chimed in. "There were a few dodgy guys in C Platoon, but, I agree, Boston was not one of them. He was never involved in any wrongdoings, and I had a lot to do with him."

"Well," Catie responded, "Apparently, a few months after they came home, Page caught Ballard with Page's wife. From what I can gather so far, Page is using his media contacts to drop feed these stories. I am leaning towards the fact that Page may be substituting Ballard's name into other real stories. Revenge can be nasty."

"Wow, that figures," said Brad. "I have heard some of these stories but had never heard Boston's name, till recently."

"One of Page's contacts is a long-time colleague of mine and he owes me," Catie said. "I will talk to him again, this time a little deeper."

"You know," said Brad, "If it's as simple as that it breaks my heart. The damage being caused by all these stories is colossal. It's bad enough for all of us when we catch our own guys responsible for these lousy acts. It really hurts when one of the good guys gets caught in the web, even if he did hump someone he shouldn't."

"But we can clear up a lot of the mud if we get to the truth," Catie ventured. "It would take the sting out of a lot of the angst people are feeling right now. I will keep on it and let you know." She got up and made ready to leave.

"Well, while you are doing that," Brad breathed in deeply as they headed to the front door, "Bert and I have talked it over. There is one really terrible story that has never come to light and has bothered us both for years, and we have decided it's time to set it right. We are well aware we should have spoken up sooner, and we also know there may be repercussions against us. There are reasons, but that is not a good enough excuse."

Catie took a deep breath. "Tell me more when we meet next week," she said, realising this was probably going to shake the Defence Force cage.

Chapter Seventeen

Detective Georgia McHenry's phone rang. "Georgia, Brian Carey. Something is happening at the Sampson office. A powder-blue Mercédes convertible has just pulled up. Two guys have gone in. I think one of them is that Alan Trundle from the Narrabeen camp. I'm not sure. I could only get a brief look."

"Do nothing. Keep watching. I'll stay on the line. We don't want to move early and risk Riley's life—that is, if he is still alive," said Georgia. "It sounds like the same Mercédes seen at the camp by the Bidvest delivery driver."

Two minutes went by during which time Georgia spread the word. Then…

"They're coming out. It is Trundle and it looks like Bushy Thompson from the Cobama gang. They have got a briefcase with them," said Carey and gave Georgia the Mercédes registration number.

"Okay. Stay on their tail. Change to Channel 17 and I will get back up. I will come out to the office now and be ready to front Sampson as soon as you get to a destination," ordered Georgia.

"Looks like they're heading back towards Parra. Changing to Channel 17 now and I will phone you when we get somewhere," Carey said as he followed them.

Georgia immediately advised VKG of the Channel change and also put out a general broadcast on Channel 33. She grabbed Detective Bruno Campbell and ran. Bruno drove. Georgia alerted Tina.

Georgia's phone rang. It was Brad Henderson. "I'm at Penno Primary with Graham following up on the Blair Chambers case. We can be at Sampson's office in five minutes if you want."

"Good, do that. Just keep an eye out that Rick doesn't go anywhere. We'll be there in around twenty minutes." She then radioed to have Parramatta police on standby.

Tina called Mike Broadfinger into the office. "I think we'd better head out there. This could develop." They headed to the basement car park and tuned in to Channel 17.

Fifteen minutes later, "Car 64 to VKG. Suspects have arrived at an industrial complex, King Solomon Importers at Norwest Business Park. Both men are going inside with the briefcase," Detective Carey radioed.

"Stay put and observe Car 64. Back up on the way and search warrant application underway," the voice ordered over the police radio soon after.

Things were hotting up. Tina decided to keep heading towards Castle Hill.

A few minutes later, "Car 64 to VKG, a black Hummer van is driving out of the loading dock. Dark windows, so we can't see who's inside," Brian Carey called in. "It could be Bushy Thompson driving."

"Car 28 to 64. We are arriving now. You can stay there and we will follow the Hummer," the Parramatta detectives replied.

"Okay. Sixty-Four out."

About five minutes later, Brad Henderson called, "Car 72 to VKG. We have got movement at the Sampson office. Rick Sampson is in his Commodore and he is heading west along Castle Hill Road. We are following."

The police radio then broadcast that information to all involved.

Two minutes later, "Car 72 to VKG. Sampson has turned left into Coonara Avenue and heading towards the Cumberland State Forest. His blinker is now on. He's about to turn into the forest. We will stay outside and go in on foot."

"Special Unit 28 to Car 72. We are following the Hummer north along Pennant Hills Road. He is heading in the general direction of the Cumberland Forest. He is now turning left into Aitken Road."

At that same time, Georgia and Bruno were arriving at the forest to join Brad. "Received that Unit 28," called Brad. "That is the back road into Cumberland Forest. We are in the bush about 100 metres from the turn into the park itself. Detective James has gone in on foot. If they come this way, don't follow them in until Detective James calls us."

"Copy that," said the Parramatta detectives.

Just then, Detective Graham James called Henderson on the two-way. "Brad. I've got a visual on Sampson. He is out of his car and waiting for someone. He is near the amenities barbecue area and he's looking nervous."

"Okay, Graham. Parra D's have just radioed. The black Hummer is coming in along Aitken Road. Stay put and keep me posted. Georgia and Bruno are here as well," Brad replied.

"Missing Persons One to Car 72," Tina called. "Brad, we are on Castle Hill Road, there in five minutes. We will stay out of sight until the Hummer goes into the park.".

"Okay chief. 72 out."

"Unit 28 to 72. Hummer is now in Coonara Road. We are pulling back as there are no other vehicles in sight."

"Okay 28. I will let you know when... hold that. We now have a visual. The black Hummer is approaching."

Brad then called on the two-way. "Gra, the black Hummer is here. We now have the chief inspector and Parra D's as well. Call me as soon as you want us in there."

The black Hummer, driven by Bushy Thompson, then turned into the forest and headed to meet Rick Sampson.

"Car 72 to Unit 28 and MP 1, Hummer is now in the forest. Please come to the turn off immediately."

Both cars did. They were there in seconds.

Detective James virtually whispered over the two way. "Brad, the Hummer is here, just pulling up. I am only one hundred metres away. They are opening the back door. Christ—it's young Riley—he's alive. He is running towards his father," he said hoarsely. "His right hand is bandaged. Otherwise he looks okay."

"Stay put, Graham. We will stop the Hummer as it leaves. You protect Riley and his father."

"Chief Inspector Samuels to VKG, instruct the raid on the Solomons Import office to go ahead *now*. Make sure all exits are covered. We want all involved. Unit 1, out."

All hell broke loose in Cumberland Forest as the Hummer disappeared back into the bush towards the entry. Bruno came out of hiding yelling, "Police. Get into the building now. Don't move out," to Riley and his father, just as shots started to ring out. Hearing the gunfire, Rick and Riley bolted for the building.

Bushy Thompson saw the police blocking the road and immediately did a U turn to go back and get hostages. Police opened fire on the Hummer as it sped off. As it drove back into the clearing, Detective James was ready, crouched behind Sampson's car. Riley and his dad were terrified and hiding in the building under a bench.

As the Hummer pulled up, Thompson saw the detective and came out firing. His accomplice was jumping out of the car as the police came from behind. Gunshots rang out. There were screams as both Thompson and his accomplice were hit. One of Thompson's shots also hit Detective James, who spun sideways and hit the ground. Georgia raced towards him.

It was over in seconds. Thompson was still alive—just. His accomplice was dead. Detective James was wounded in the shoulder and Georgia made him comfortable. Tina yelled at Brad to get ambulances and raced into the building. Riley and his father were both safe and unhurt.

"It's okay, Riley. Everything is over," said the chief inspector soothingly to a frightened and teary seven-year-old. "You are going to be just fine." She then noticed blood on the kid's bandages.

Tina ordered Rick and Riley to wait inside until the ambulances arrived and everything was secure. She then quietly told Georgia not to handcuff Rick in front of his son. "But keep a close eye on him."

Meanwhile, at the Norwest Business Park, sirens blared as police cars and unmarked vehicles came from every direction. Solomons Imports was surrounded. Police came in from front and back screaming at everyone to get down.

One loading dock employee made a run for it but the police dogs had him down in seconds. He was screaming. One detective murmured to him, "Looks like your arse will be sore for some time creep," as he locked the handcuffs on before shackling his legs.

Police tasered another, who ran at them with his knife drawn. He looked like he was high on something but they got him down, text book style. Otherwise the whole operation was over in a few minutes. Eighteen people were quickly in custody, including the two brought down by dogs and taser.

"Hey, Inspector," one of the Parra D's yelled to Inspector Derek Sward. "We've found a well set-up SP bookies room. Looks like an upmarket TAB on steroids. This is a big operation."

The inspector was in the main office and was troubled. They had found no brief case. That seemed odd. The squad was searching the building and he hoped they might find it elsewhere.

Detective Carey spoke. "Well, Mr Trundle. We meet again. You're a long way from Narrabeen Lakes Youth Camp and my guess is you won't be back there for many years. That will depend on just how co-operative you are." He sat a whimpering, handcuffed Trundle down at a desk.

"They made me do it. I had no choice," choked Trundle in a whining voice. "They threatened my wife and kids if I didn't co-operate."

"Who are they?"

"The boss, Lofty Atkins," whimpered Trundle. "He and Squizzy Taylor bolted down their secret passage as soon as they got a phone call, about thirty seconds before we heard the sirens coming." He was almost in tears.

"Hey Inspector, the two main hoods have scampered," called Carey to Inspector Sward, dragging Trundle into the office. Show us the secret passage Trundle." Brian then gave the escaped mobsters' names to the Inspector, who knew them both. Trundle didn't know how it worked. He pointed to a bookshelf. "It's there somewhere. I saw it open," he mumbled.

The detectives soon wheeled in a thirtyish girl with bright pink hair. "This is Helena. She knows the drill," said a plain clothes detective.

"Show us how it works, Helena" the Inspector ordered. She pressed the button behind the left-hand book end and the door opened. Two police went in, guns drawn, and disappeared down the well-lit passageway.

Meantime, back in the warehouse, the storage areas were yielding lots of treasure.

"You can bet your boots this is all stolen property," ventured one detective, looking at a huge stock of cartons containing everything from computers and flat screen TVs to cosmetics, alcohol, cigarettes, guns and spare parts.

They found another area stacked full of various drugs. "Phew. Look at that. There's a few bobs worth there," said a uniformed senior sergeant. It turned out to be over forty-million-dollars-worth, just in that room alone.

Chief Inspector Samuels and Mike Broadfinger arrived and were immediately briefed by Derek Sward. He told Tina the two ringleaders had got away in a black Audi. They had received a warning phone call. "I have issued an all-points bulletin on the Audi and the two men. It can be assumed they took the briefcase," he said.

The secret passageway had exited at the next-door Coles Service Station. It came out at the fence behind a large commercial gas tank where they had a camouflaged gate. The attendant had seen them running and driving off very fast. He took down the registration number, as he thought they may have not paid for fuel.

"The PA also showed us the wall safe over here," Derek Sward showed Tina. "It's huge and we will need to get it opened by locksmiths. From what we have gathered, they didn't have time to open it themselves. Looks like they just grabbed the briefcase and bolted. This is a humongous operation."

The inspector went on, "By the way, your man, Detective Carey, and his sidekick, did a brilliant job. They had a battle plan ready as soon as we all arrived and it worked like a charm."

"Thanks Derek," said Tina "I'll leave all this to you and your team. It's going to take a while. I'm going back to Chatswood to wind up the Riley Sampson kidnapping and report to Commissioner Palmer to get him off my back. I'll call you later and we can meet up."

"Sure, Tina. Just yell out whenever you are ready, day or night." Tina and the inspector had worked together on many cases and were a mutual admiration society.

Tina then sought out Detective Carey. "Great job, Brian. You've done us proud. This is going to take some time to wind up. Riley is safe. He and his dad are on their way to Chatswood and a medical examination.

Graham James was wounded in the gun battle at Cumberland Forest but will be okay. He is in Hornsby Hospital. Bushy Thompson is fighting for his life. No loss there. His accomplice is dead. We are waiting on identification. Mike, Georgia, Graham, Brad and Bruno were brilliant under pressure. It's been a good result. This warehouse is a huge bonus. What a finish." She was stating the obvious.

"I'm going back to Chatswood. You two stay here under Inspector Sward. Try to keep the media at bay as much as possible. I will see you back at Chatswood when you finish. Tell your respectives it will be a late night. Again, thanks for a top effort."

She and Mike headed for the car just as another ambulance arrived. Tina phoned the commissioner, Catie and, later, David. Mike drove.

CHAPTER EIGHTEEN

Tina made herself a strong black coffee as she arrived at Chatswood HQ. The whole building was buzzing. "Well done, Sir," called Bryce Rixon as she walked past. Word had soon got round that Riley was okay. Case solved. Victory all round.

Georgia was the first into her office to update Tina.

"Riley's mum, Jan, is here with our community team and Riley in the upstairs lounge. Riley is okay, but the mob sure showed what arseholes they are. They had his finger amputated and delivered to his father as an incentive to pay up. How rough is that? A little kid.

"Rick Sampson is a mess. He is now in the interview room with Brad and Bruno. He's being very co-operative. I venture this may have cured his gambling addiction, but what a price! It sounds like he has taken most of the $200,000 out of his real estate trust funds, illegally, to repay his gambling debt to the Cobama mob. His brother-in-law is Bushy Thompson. Thompson and Alan Trundle orchestrated Riley's abduction. Riley has been at the Norwest Business Park office for the past five weeks. It seems Trundle was also in debt to the mob and he helped Thompson tie and gag Riley at Narrabeen and then put him into the boot of the Mercedes."

"Georgia, when all the dust settles," said Inspector Samuels, "We are going out for a flash dinner. Just you and I. All I can say right now is a huge thank you. Your intuition and skills combined to deliver a fantastic result. We are the pride of the force today, thanks to you. Not only Riley's safe return but the dismantling of a major organised crime gang."

Tina then briefed the detective on what was happening at Norwest and what had been uncovered. "Can you organise to get the team together at say, six, then a media briefing in the conference room at six-thirty? I will take it. That will lead into the late news. I'll do a brief report for the commissioner then, straight after the media scrum, I will head out to Hornsby Hospital to see Graham."

Georgia floated out of Tina's office feeling very satisfied, but totally exhausted.

Tina finished the report for Commissioner Palmer and sent it through just after five thirty. She had outlined the activities at Sampson's office, the Cumberland Forest and the Norwest Business Park. She reported on the death of one mobster plus the wounding of another, and also the shooting of Detective James and the escape of the two gang leaders.

The report also summarised Riley's abduction, the finger amputation, the ransom demands and the missing trust funds, plus a brief inventory of what had been uncovered at the warehouse. Tina advised that she was working with Inspector Sward and promised a full report within twenty-four hours. She told of the media briefing called for six-thirty, and said she would be heading out to Hornsby Hospital after that.

Mike Broadfinger popped his head in. "You're going to love this chief. I've just heard from the Ds at Parra that one name keeps coming up in the interviews. It seems Jim Heggarty was also Waldron's bagman for the Cobama gang. The boy gets around. He was a regular at their Norwest HQ."

"You've got to be kidding. How did we not know?" sighed Tina.

"On another matter, Tina," Mike said gently, "now that we have wrapped this… your health. I know it's not my right to pry, but I would like to help. Anything. Just ask and I'll be there."

"Thanks, Mike. The trouble is that you and I both know that today is just the tip of the iceberg. We have much bigger and more dangerous challenges ahead. I am due for more treatment in the coming weeks that may knock me around a little. I'll keep you in the loop. Promise."

Just before six, Tina's phone rang. "Hi, Commissioner," she answered.

"Call me John, Tina. I know you are flat out. I just wanted to say congratulations to you and your team. A great day. I'll see you at the task force meeting on Wednesday, and look forward to your report tomorrow. Well done," said the commissioner genuinely.

Tina had time for a quick call to Inspector Sward. "Derek, I'm buggered. I've got a team meeting in two minutes, a media briefing at six-thirty, then I'm heading to Hornsby Hospital to see Graham. Can we meet tomorrow, say around nine a.m.? Is that okay?"

"Yeah, Tina. Sure thing. I am still here at Norwest. We have really uncovered a hornet's nest. It's bigger than we thought. How about nine at my office. We'll have all the backup info we need there."

"Done. See you at Parra at nine," said Tina.

The buzz in the team meeting was palpable. Tina outlined the full day's events, Georgia's input and the tremendous teamwork. She advised that Graham James was on the mend and singled out Brad and Bruno for their skills and co-ordination. Tina congratulated Brian Carey in his absence and thanked Sergeant Bryce Rixon for holding the fort together at HQ during all the mayhem.

Tina finished with, "The bottom line is that Riley is safe and will be home with his Mum tonight. Case closed, a great result. The bonus is that we have uncovered a massive organised crime operation and will, hopefully, have it totally closed down within days and the mob locked up for many years. There will be kids alive next year who will have no idea we have saved them." She smiled. "That's life. Well done all. I will need all your reports on my desk by Monday, mid-afternoon. Enjoy your weekend. You all deserve it."

They filed out of the room in a cheerful mood.

The media briefing started off mildly, but quickly descended into a rowdy session. Tina opened with the same pitch that she had used to close the team meeting. "The best news I have is that young Riley Sampson is safe and well and will be home with his mum and grandparents tonight."

She then went on to briefly outline the day's activities, concluding with, "As you would appreciate, we have a huge job ahead of us to wind up our investigations, and there are sensitive things I am not at liberty to discuss due to the ongoing nature of the investigations. I will be in a position to elaborate further on these matters early next week. I just want to say how proud I am of the Missing Persons team and the Police from Parramatta for such a great result today. Any questions?"

"Have you caught the two ringleaders who escaped?" was the first one.

"No. We have very strong leads, and we are confident of early arrests."

"Can you name them, so the public can help?"

"As I said, we do have strong leads as to their whereabouts, but I am not at liberty to name anyone at this stage."

"Was Riley's father involved with the kidnapping?" This came from the back of the room.

"Riley's father is helping us with our enquiries. It is too early to say anything else."

From the ABC journo near the front, "Did the police over react, shooting one man dead and wounding another after Riley's safe release?"

"All I can tell you is that it appears the gang members fired on police, wounding one detective. The police response was immediate and successful."

"Did you have to set the dogs onto an employee of the Import Business?"

And so it went on…

Tina called a halt to the briefing just after seven p.m. It had gone as expected. They are never a pleasant encounter, even when you win. She thought all her answers were in line with police procedures.

As she drove up the Pacific Highway, Tina phoned Catie to fill her in. "We've just seen you on the ABC Breaking News. Congratulations. Alvaro and I were watching it. I've just left him."

"Alvaro?"

"Yep," Catie replied, "the Colombian fisherman and I have caught up already. He's a nice guy. All is good here. We can't wait to see you."

"How did Alvaro react to the news about Nick?'

"Devastated, blames himself. He has taken it very personally, but the good news is it has only strengthened his resolve to beat these mongrels."

"Well, things are moving fast down here. I have another treatment on Tuesday then a high-level task force meeting on our case, Wednesday. I hope to be up there Thursday or Friday. I'll let you know."

"Great. My next treatment is on Tuesday as well. I should be fine from Thursday onwards. I want to introduce you to a couple of people.

How long can you stay?" asked Catie.

"Maybe overnight and back next day? I can't be away too long," Tina responded.

"Okay. I think you'll be pleasantly surprised."

Tina asked her to keep Anita in the loop and to check up on her. They hung up just as Tina was arriving at Hornsby Hospital. She hoped they would let her in. It was right on eight p.m.

Chapter Nineteen

The next week was a blur.

Tina and Inspector Sward spent half a day together on the Saturday preparing a joint report to go to Commissioner Palmer. Derek reported that a number of the Cobama mobsters' employees became very co-operative. Two more warehouses were located overnight. A number of homes were raided in the morning. There were more arrests pending.

So far, the team had recovered a huge drug haul, a large cache of fire arms—including AK 47s—over eight-hundred-thousand dollars in cash, a number of stolen prestige cars and a staggering amount of stolen property. Plus, they now had an extensive list of the mob's contacts. This was all on top of the elaborate SP bookmaking set up.

"We even have the name of the medic who took off Riley's pinky," Inspector Sward reported. "At this point we have thirty-eight people in custody with more to come and some good leads on both Atkins and Taylor. Seems they have gone their separate ways. We think Atkins is in Melbourne."

They discussed the list of names and roles that had come out of the many interviews and property searches. Two of the police names, as expected, were Waldron and Heggarty, but a couple were surprises to Tina and Derek. There were no surprises in the political names.

"Leave that to me, Derek," said Tina. "I can say there is another operation going on that I am involved with and this info needs to be kept under wraps at the moment."

Tina left Derek in charge to mop up. He would have a big task but was well up to it. This freed Tina to work on other matters, including her treatment.

On Sunday night, acting on a tip off, Darlinghurst Police raided one of the mob's clubs at Kings Cross and arrested Squizzy Taylor in the back rooms. Taylor was filthy. One down, one to go, but no briefcase.

On a very hectic Monday, Tina had a number of key meetings. She and Mike Broadfinger spent two hours working out how to wrap up the Riley Sampson case and push forward on the big one. Mike was given the task of finalising the Sampson report. He had spent most of Sunday with Rick Sampson. As expected, Sampson had capitulated to the mob completely when Riley's finger was delivered to his office along with a recording of the screams of his little boy as the procedure took place. He had received a call from the mob about his gambling debt two days after Riley went missing. He had been trying to get money together ever since. He sold his Audi and was now driving the office Commodore. He sold his power boat and two jet skis, amongst others, all at fire-sale prices. He had sought help from friends with little result. In desperation, he had taken $115,000 from his clients' trust funds to make up the $200,000 required.

Sampson had not met Alan Trundle until that Friday at his office, but he had been involved in a number of dealings with his brother-in-law, Bushy Thompson, over the years. They were not close.

Tina pointed out that Taskforce Delta would now wind up and therefore free up all involved. They decided to pick the best for their new team to assist 'Taskforce Cleanout'. They selected Detectives Georgia McHenry, Brian Carey, Graham James, Bruno Campbell and Brad Henderson, plus desk Sergeant Bryce Rixon. Mike was to organise a meeting for three p.m. on Wednesday, after Tina's meeting with the commissioner.

"I might also run it past Inspector Sward at Parra. He would be an asset and has instant access to a big squad." Tina then summoned Detective Henderson to her office. "Shut the door Brad." She motioned him to sit down.

"What's up, Chief" asked Brad.

Tina firstly re-iterated her congratulations from last Friday's meeting, then updated him on all that had transpired in the Sampson/Cobama case. She then said, "Brad, we have been together a long time and I must confess there have been times over the past month when I have doubted your commitment to the team and also your work ethic. Is there something wrong? Have we done something to upset you?"

Brad became edgy. "What have I done wrong? I've done everything you've asked. Where did I let the team down?" he asked tersely.

"This has nothing to do with who is right or wrong, Brad. I say again, you and I have been together a long while and I can pick when something's wrong. Whatever it is, I just called you in to see if I could help," said Tina calmly.

She could see Brad was wrestling with something in his head. "Can I get us a coffee?"

Brad nodded. When Tina got back, Brad let it all out.

"Nita left me five weeks ago. She took the kids and has gone to live with her mum and dad in Padstow," he said sadly. "It's killing me. I'm alone in a four-bedroom house, miserable, and trying hard to stay away from the pub. I just don't know where to turn."

Tina thought for a few seconds and then asked, "Is it anything to do with work? The odd hours or the long days? That must make it tough."

"I guess that's part of it. I have missed a few things at the kids' school that I promised to go to, and Nita has been caught in all their sports transport and social needs. But it has been building for a while and it's not all work."

"Have you sought out some sort of counselling or mediation?"

"Not really. There hasn't been much time lately. I guess we should have done that way back. I don't know if it would help or not."

"Have you seen Nita or the kids since?"

"Yeah, her folks are great people and have invited me over for dinner a couple of nights every week," Brad said. "That is the only thing keeping me sane."

"And how is Nita at those dinners?"

"Okay. We talk civilly and she hasn't poisoned me with the kids, thank God. They're devastated. I think she wants to work it out. I just don't know."

"Well, I'd love to help in any way possible, including a sit down with Nita if that would assist." Tina smiled. "Nita and I have always got on very well."

"Thanks Chief, and thanks for listening. I'll let you know if I need anything. I am going over to Padstow tonight."

"Two quick things then. I would love you to be at a meeting Mike will tell you about. Wednesday, three p.m., here at Chatswood. Also, school holidays in two weeks. If you want time off for a break with your family—just yell," Tina said as they parted. She felt Brad was pleased to get it off his chest and Tina was also glad it wasn't something wrong at work.

Later that afternoon, Tina drove up the highway, first to visit Graham at Hornsby Hospital and later to see how Riley was settling in back at home.

Graham James advised he looked like being discharged in two days and could be back at work on light duties within a couple of weeks. He was chuffed when Tina told him of his new assignment. "I'd love to be there Wednesday," he chirped.

Riley was really enjoying being back home and getting loads of attention. He was looking forward to seeing all his school friends again. He was going back on Wednesday, after all the medical appointments had been completed. His mum, Jan, was deeply thankful.

"Inspector, I must confess there were times when we didn't think we'd see Riley again," she had confided. "And now, all he wants is show and tell at school."

"If it makes you feel any better—that's two of us," said Tina. "Every one of my team is as thankful as you are, and we sure got more than we bargained for."

Tina had responded openly to Jan's questions about Rick and what was likely to happen to him. Tina sensed she still had hopes he would survive all this and eventually get on with his life. Tina admired her forgiveness. That, certainly, was not the thinking of Jan's parents. They had made that clear.

Tuesday found Tina back at the San for chemotherapy. So far, she had not lost her hair and had pulled up okay from her Tuesday 'milkshake'. She had a few headaches and felt tired, but she was thankful, as others seemed to be a lot worse off. Dr. Emslie thought that all the adrenalin responses to her work challenges were helping Tina through it.

David had, again, driven her today and stayed throughout the procedure. They stopped off at Flower Power, their favourite nursery, for a lazy, late lunch. When they returned home Tina made a few calls to catch up with things and then booked her own flights up Thursday afternoon, returning from the Gold Coast Friday morning.

She then rang Catie to let her know arrival details before settling down for a rare, quiet night with David.

Wednesday was a big one. Tina went in early to prepare for the task force meeting at ten and also for her own team's get together at three p.m. Both were important happenings and things should be a lot clearer tonight. She arrived at the Leagues Club right on ten.

After the obligatory handshakes, greetings, and getting a coffee, Commissioner Palmer asked them to sit down. He welcomed everyone around the table and started by congratulating Tina and her team on solving the Riley Sampson abduction and also on the dismantling of the Cobama gang network.

"On that front, I have some breaking news. Lofty Atkins was taken into custody in Melbourne about an hour ago. He still had the briefcase and most of the cash. Rick Sampson will be happy to hear that. I thank Rusty for his assistance in locating both Taylor and Atkins."

Rusty nodded.

The commissioner went on to pull together all the information gathered from Catie, Alvaro, Heggarty and Anita. He added a lot more that had since been uncovered by Alan MacDonald, Warren Hardcastle and Rusty's networks. It was a sobering picture.

Summing up, John Palmer said, "So, we know that a monster drug shipment is to leave Colombia in just over two weeks. We know the ship, and—thanks to Alan's Colombian counterpart—we know the intended route and destination port, which is now Newcastle, not Sydney. We also know the intended transfer details of the drugs into the Moriarty mob's warehouse complex at the Sydney markets. We still have a few gaps to fill around the Newcastle Port operation and Border Force activities. Alan is on top of that. We will get the names of all involved before the shipment arrives."

"What we now need to do is work out how and where we intercept the shipment to maximise our aims to catch the whole gang and uncover their distribution channels."

The team then spent time discussing various options, the compilation of their troops and the many obstacles they could encounter. Tina had suggested pulling Anita and her little girl and getting them into a safe house. The commissioner had disagreed. "Her disappearance would alert the mob that something was wrong. We need her at the coal face until the shipment leaves the wharves."

They spent time discussing the arrest of crooked police and politicians—including the new names from this week's Cobama gang interviews—and where to incarcerate them.

"This is going to shake a few establishments around the world right to the core, including senior judiciary figures," Deputy Commissioner MacDonald ventured.

"Here's hoping," replied John Palmer, "but our plan and paperwork has to be flawless. That is a big challenge in itself."

The meeting broke up just after noon, with everyone aware of their individual responsibilities. They would meet same time, same place next Wednesday, unless something urgent came up in the meantime. The commissioner was pleased to hear about Tina's new team for this operation but warned her against telling them too much yet.

As Tina drove over the Harbour Bridge even she was in awe of the Taskforce's progress and the mammoth challenge ahead. She feared for Catie, Anita and Alvaro. She was not as charitable with Heggarty and his cohorts.

The three p.m. meeting created a buzz of excitement with the new team. Everyone was delighted that Graham James had made it—direct from his hospital bed.

"Wouldn't miss it for quids. Just don't touch my busted wing."

Chief Inspector Samuels welcomed the new team. "I am pleased to say that Inspector Sward will be joining us next week and also delighted that Graham is out of hospital and here with us." Derek Sward had been more than happy to be involved. Tina had briefed him fully and asked him to keep it under wraps for the moment.

Tina then went on to announce the formation of Taskforce Cleanout and congratulated them for being selected. She had been vague on detail and about the task ahead. No names and no specifics. "The final plans are being formulated as we speak. It is a big operation and I will be in a position to give you full details when we meet again next Monday at ten a.m. The purpose of today is to get you all to clear your desks, have a bit of time off and get ready for the new challenge."

The new team were keen to learn details of the new case and already looking forward to whatever it was. Both Bruno and Graham had asked about Jim Heggarty, as they had both worked closely with him in 'Delta', and everyone knew something was amiss.

"Heggarty has some issues. It was Jim putting those stories out to the media. He is currently on stress leave and not contactable," was all Tina offered, and no more was said. "So, until Monday, not a word to a soul, including those at home. The last thing we want to do is put those we love most in the firing line. We are dealing with the scum of the earth, who think nothing of pulling the trigger."

She went on to talk about Nick Pashilidis, whom some of them knew. "Nick died on suspicion. They thought he may know something. But he didn't."

Earlier that week, Tina had gone to Nick's funeral. It was well attended, as he was very popular and highly respected by many at the markets as well as those in his own community at Ryde. His wife and three children were totally devastated. Quite a few of the police who had worked with Nick were there, and Tina was pleased she went. She had seen Carlos Carezo and Dave Gillespie in the crowd and stayed well clear of them, avoiding any contact.

After the new task force meeting Tina went back to her office and called in Mike Broadfinger. "Mike , I'm heading out overnight to see Alvaro and Catie. I will be flying back tomorrow at eleven a.m. I need you to pick me up at the airport." She gave Mike the flight details. "No one needs to know I'm away, or where," she concluded.

"Sure chief," Mike replied.

By the time Tina arrived at the airport she just wanted to relax and chill out. It had been a challenging week.

Chapter Twenty

Tina emerged from the arrival tunnel and waved to Catie. As she only had hand luggage, they went straight to the Gold Coast Airport car park for the thirty-minute drive to Alvaro's canal-front safe house.

Tina turned on her phone, just one message. Mike. "Please phone ASAP."

She rang his mobile. "Hi Mike. What's up?"

"Boss, we may have a problem. Pat Waldron is raising the roof about Jim Heggarty. He says Jim has some vital information on a case he is working on. He has enlisted the support of Deputy Commissioner Kel Mackay, who rang me about an hour ago."

"So, what did you say?"

"I told Waldron exactly what you said at the meeting, and I told the deputy commissioner we had it under control. No more. He was not happy."

"Okay. Tread carefully. See you at the airport tomorrow morning."

Tina was worried. *Why was Mackay involved?* She had always thought well of him.

As they drove, Catie filled Tina in on Alvaro. "He has settled in well. Loves his fishing, but is kind of edgy. Things are going too slowly for him."

Tina could understand that. Nothing to do; too much time to think. Hopefully it would be over soon.

Catie continued. "Also, Anita Collins came up to Brisbane to see her mum last weekend for a long overdue visit. I caught up with her for about an hour or so. She is one tough cookie. She still seems happy to be doing some good but is nervous. She told me the mob are worried that a detective contact, Jim Heggarty, has gone missing. She also told me they still have another contact in Taskforce Delta but she didn't get a name. I promised to talk to her tomorrow morning after your visit. She will call from a phone box."

Tina tensed. *Another mole? Surely not?* She hoped Anita was wrong.

Tina hardly recognised Alvaro as they walked into his unit. No beard and now blonde. What a difference. She told him, and Alvaro laughed.

"I see myself in the mirror and have to look twice," he said.

They made tea and coffee then sat on the front porch overlooking the canal, munching biscuits. Alvaro proudly showed off some bream and flathead he had caught.

Tina told them both about how the Riley Sampson case had wound up and how they had completely dismantled the Cobama gang operation. "It was way bigger than we thought."

She then told them about Nick Pashilidi's funeral and the huge turnout. She could see that Alvaro was still very affected. His eyes hardened when Tina said that Carezo and Gillespie were there.

Tina then opened up and related all the collective new information they had on the Moriarty mob, the massive drug shipment, and all the distribution and storage details. There were absolutely no worries about telling these two. They had more to fear from the mob than anyone else—except, perhaps, Anita.

Both Alvaro and Catie were very impressed with how much detail the police had accumulated. Alvaro was particularly pleased about how his own information was valuable and fitted in. "They must have received a lot more information from the Colombian end?" he ventured.

"We did, and that brings me to the next important point. Deputy Commissioner MacDonald has impeccable contacts on the ground there, including one in the La Cometa Gallery in Bogota where Olga is a Director on the board. Your message will be delivered safely in the next few days," said Tina.

Alvaro was extremely happy to hear this, and asked, "Will Olga be able to respond?"

"It should be possible."

Alvaro already knew Olga was on the gallery board. He had read it in his weekly *City Paper Bogota*. The gallery had been founded by Esteban Jarmillo, a friend of his family.

They talked on until Catie said, "I am working on another case at the moment—a story about the Australian SAS Commandos in Afghanistan and possible war crimes. Plus, I have reconnected with an amazing and successful corporate guru at my radiation clinic. I really want you two to meet these very special people. I have organised dinner at six-thirty p.m. I hope that's okay?"

Tina responded, "It will do us good to do something normal. You had better take me to my hotel so I can shower and change. It's been a long day."

The first thing Tina did after checking in was to ring Mike with Anita's news that the mob still had a contact in 'Delta'. Mike was surprised. They discussed it in detail but came up with a blank.

"Whatever happens, we need to find out quickly, if possible before our meeting on Monday with the new team," Tina warned. They agreed to discuss it further tomorrow.

The dinner got off to a lively start. Tina was immediately impressed with Catie's contacts. The man-mountain—SAS Commando, Brad Spruce, and his wife Jane, were delightful and she recognised Garth Peterson from his many media features. Garth and his wife Meg were modest, and Tina really liked their openness. It was obvious Garth and Meg were a dynamic partnership and had done extremely well as a result.

Catie had found a quiet corner in a delightful little Thai house in Broadbeach. At the end of their third bottle of Marlborough Sound Sauvignon Blanc, and some delicious food, the table was buzzing. Alvaro proclaimed it was the best night he had ever had in Australia. By night's end, they had solved all the world's problems, and happily agreed to do it all again at the first opportunity.

Garth picked up the bill and they went their separate ways.

CHAPTER TWENTY-ONE

Sydney airport was buzzing as always. Mike and Tina sat in the airport coffee lounge to discuss plans. Tina told Mike about the day and night. They had just started discussing the Delta team when Tina's phone rang. She looked at the face and said, "I'd better take this." She swiped the answer button. "Hi, Catie. That was quick. Did I leave something behind?"

"Tina, I just got off the phone to Anita. She rang early because she overheard Tony talking this morning. They found out today that you have been to the Gold Coast. They think that is where Heggarty might be hidden."

Tina went cold. The only two people who knew where she was were her hubby, David, and Mike. "Thanks, Catie. I'll call you back," she said flatly. She was thinking at one-hundred miles an hour.

Mike could see Tina was troubled. "You look puzzled?"

"Mike, this is really important and please, be one hundred percent sure with your answer. Have you told anyone at all, even your family, that I was on the Gold Coast?"

Mike responded immediately. "No way. Why would I?" he said abruptly, but then, after a brief pause, "except Bryce Rixon this morning, but the sarge is okay."

Tina breathed out a real sigh of relief. "That was Catie to tell me the Moriartys found out this morning that I was on the Gold Coast and that's where they think we've stashed Heggarty. Thank God we have found the leak."

She felt lucky.

"Holy Toledo," said Mike." I just can't see Rixon being on their team. God, I'm sorry," he said. "He just casually asked me where you'd been when I left to pick you up."

"If you'd told him yesterday, they would have followed me and we would have blown Alvaro and Catie's whereabouts. They would both be dead by now."

Tina let that sink in.

They discussed a plan to isolate the desk sergeant from Monday's briefing and how maybe they could use the situation to their advantage. They needed to get access to his phone and computer data. As Mike drove out of the airport, they did not notice the black sedan pulling out to follow them.

"We are close to Heggarty's safe house," said Mike. "Do you need to ask him anything?"

Tina thought it over. "Nah, we'd better get straight to HQ. I've got a lot on," she replied not realising what a good decision that was.

Tina made herself a strong black coffee before heading to her office. She nodded and smiled as normal to Desk Sergeant Rixon's greeting but did not engage in any conversation. *Life's full of surprises,* she thought to herself.

Her mind wandered back to last night's dinner. She should do things like that more often. Great people and really good company. Catie sure had some fabulous connections. She googled Garth Peterson and was even more impressed when she saw his corporate, community and philanthropic history. She then googled Brad Spruce, but nothing came up. *SAS—should have realised that,* she thought to herself. If she had put in 'Sergeant S' she may have seen his Victoria Cross Award.

Tina spent the next half hour going over Inspector Sward's report on the Colombian gang before calling Brad Henderson in to wrap up the Riley Sampson case. Under normal circumstances, she would have been basking in the glow of success. Two major cases with really successful closes, but Tina was feeling uneasy about the next major challenge. She was really worried about Alvaro, Anita and Catie.

Brad opened up by informing Tina that he and Nita had agreed to seek counselling and had taken up her suggestion. They had booked a week-long holiday at Laurieton, near Port Macquarie, in the school holidays. Tina approved his leave application and wished them well.

It was early afternoon when Tina's desk phone rang. "Commissioner Palmer is here in reception. He is asking if you are available," said Bryce Rixon.

"Of course, bring him up," said Tina immediately, and Brad disappeared.

She was pleased. It was a chance to bring the commissioner up to date with her misgivings. Tina welcomed him and organised coffee for both of them. After the coffees arrived, she shut the door and started to talk.

The commissioner was taken aback when told about Bryce Rixon. "I've worked with Bryce for years and just said g'day to him downstairs. He has always been a role model for the junior ranks. A terrific bloke. That really surprises me," he said.

Tina told him she'd plan to put Rixon on a last-minute surveillance job on Monday to keep him away from the new task-force meeting. Her plan was to brief him separately later and to pass on some sort of misinformation to the mob to try to expose him.

"I hope Mike Broadfinger learned a valuable lesson," the commissioner said. He then went on to tell Tina of their new information on the Newcastle Wharf connections. "We've hit the jackpot. We now have most of the key people fingered. All we need is to get it right and keep it under wraps. But I also wanted to tell you that Alvaro's message to his wife was really well received yesterday. Apparently, Olga burst into tears and took some time to settle. She has been fearing the worst for a long time. She will be giving our contact a reply very soon."

The commissioner then outlined a plan they had concocted. Olga had recently done a very successful speaking tour around Colombia, Venezuela, Ecuador and Brazil for the Cometa Gallery. "We think we can organise one for Australia and New Zealand. What do you think?" he asked.

"Fantastic. I cannot even imagine how Alvaro would feel if it comes off," said Tina. She then decided it was right to bring the commissioner up to date on her health issues. He showed real concern.

"Tina, above all, you owe it to yourself to do your utmost to get on top of this. There are enough of us to fill the gap to allow you time off to do your best."

"Thanks, but no. My doctors are telling me that the work challenges are keeping my mind off it and that is a positive. And I am pacing myself with regular breaks when I feel down. Mike covers for me every time, and David is amazing."

"Okay, your call. Just do what's best for you."

The commissioner then went on to tell Tina that next Wednesday's meeting would have two new faces, because they needed to plan a military style operation to seize the drug shipment. "We now know there are also guns, ammunition and other gems in the shipment."

After the commissioner had gone, Tina called Mike into her office and they spent a long time going over every detail to make sure they missed nothing. "I am going to try to have a break this weekend. I've got a feeling we may not get another for quite some time. I'm going to talk David into a trip south," Tina said as they were finishing up.

"Good for you. See you first thing Monday," said Mike as he left.

Chapter Twenty-Two

Catie was smiling to herself. It had been a few busy but productive days. Tina's visit had certainly lifted Alvaro's spirits. The dinner, too, had gone way above her highest expectations. She felt there had been a real bonding.

Catie had spent the weekend with Brad and Jane Spruce and his colleague, Bert Hunter, trying to piece together the harrowing tale of their time in Uruzgan Province in Afghanistan. It had obviously taken a huge toll on both of them over the years.

"I didn't see it coming," Brad had said. "We were on the chopper one night, heading to Panwa Village from Tarinkot. We had been briefed on the possible presence of Abdul Haja Rofellah—a senior Taliban recruiter. The major seemed edgy but that's all, and it was not uncommon.

"We hit the ground running and came into the village from the south. I heard the gunfire and screams coming from the small Mosque, but by the time I arrived they were all dead—seven men and boys. They were all unarmed and had been praying. Major Ramsay was planting pistols, a camera and a radio on the oldest men. He was shaking. It was then that I realised he was high on something."

Bert the chimed in. "I came in from the west side door of the Mosque and saw the carnage. The major told us they had fired on him as he came in. That's crap. None of them were armed. The troops then went house to house as planned and, the good news was, we captured not only Rofellah, but two of his senior aides. That was a major coup for us." They had then shackled the prisoners and loaded them into the chopper.

Back at the base, Brad and Bert had agonised over their report. The major had made it very clear to both of them that they would be in for a rough ride if they didn't back his story. Given little choice, they complied. But here they were, years later. Major General Chris Ramsay was now OIC of the fourth brigade command force in charge of Australian intelligence surveillance, based at Victoria Barracks in Sydney. He was among the top brass in the Army.

Both the boys were sickened with the thought of what had transpired in Uruzgan Province years earlier.

"How many others could corroborate your story," asked Catie.

The boys came up with three names. "Angus Stewart is now out and living at Bathurst, but I think Harry Margiotta and Todd Mason are still active," Brad told her. They gave her as many details as they could.

"The real tragedy here is that we did so many great things on our three tours, yet it makes me sick to think about this. We developed great friendships with our Afghan interpreters and citizens," said Bert.

They then told Catie about Jumali Qasam, a key interpreter who was fiercely loyal to the Australian troops. So much so the Taliban had put a big price on his head.

"Jumali is still in the refugee centre here at Villawood and looks like being sent back," said Brad. "I can't work us out. Here's a bloke who put his life on the line for us so many times. Yet, here we are about to send him back to almost certain torture and death. It doesn't make sense… any of it."

Both Brad and Bert were visibly moved by all this. Catie promised she would do her level best to get as much detail as possible, and that she would then work out a plan with them to try to rectify some of the wrongdoings.

On Tuesday, Catie again ran into Garth at the radiation clinic. Garth had been really pleased with the dinner.

"We can't thank you enough. Meg and I went home with renewed faith in the world. Brad, Tina and Alvaro were a breath of fresh air."

Catie hung around after her treatment. When Garth came out, she asked could they have coffee together. She explained to Garth that she needed advice 'and a miracle'. She told him of Brad and Bert's Afghanistan experience and her need to try to get the other three to corroborate their story. "But, most of all, I need an extremely senior, decent and powerful defence force officer prepared to help us expose this dreadful cover up," said Catie

Garth smiled. "Then, this is your lucky day," he said, and went on to tell Catie of his great mate, honest as the day is long and as tough as nails.

"And he just happens to be chief of the Australian Defence Force."

Yes, it had been a productive few days. Catie could afford to smile.

Chapter Twenty-Three

David and Tina couldn't remember when they last had such a great weekend. Leaving Sydney on Friday arvo, they had arrived at Mossy Point around seven p.m. Their holiday 'shack' on Annetts Parade backed on to the beautiful Tomaga River. They had fallen in love with it at first sight years ago.

David immediately got the fire going while Tina unpacked and heated up the casserole she brought from Sydney. They opened a special Barossa Merlot and drank it. After dinner they sat in front of the crackling winter fire and Tina told David about the dinner at Broadbeach. They went to bed listening to the rolling surf.

"After all this over, I am taking you up to meet them. What a great bunch of people," Tina told him. They talked long into the night, in a very positive way, about their future.

Waking up to the chortling sound of magpies and the sun's rays filtering through the trees and reflecting off the calm blue water was heaven. After scrambled eggs and bacon, they dragged the tinny out from under, grabbed the fishing gear and hit the river. David rowed, and soon caught a large silver bream near the mangrove roots.

"Dinner, fresh as you can get," he bragged.

Later that day, they walked hand in hand down to Candlagan Creek Lagoon and paddled in the sandy, clear water, marvelling how warm it was for August. Life could not have been better. Neither wanted to leave on Sunday, but duty called. So, after waving to Poo Bear's Cave on the Clyde Mountain and a mandatory stop at Braidwood Bakery, they travelled north on the Hume and back to Epping. Tina caught the Metro to Chatswood on Monday morning and felt a million dollars.

"No need to ask how the weekend went. It's written all over your face," Mike said as he came into her office. Tina smiled.

Just after nine, Tina called Bryce Rixon into her office.

"Sorry, Bryce, something has just come up and I need you to stake out a tattoo parlour in North Sydney now. Our intel advises there is to be a meeting there and I need photos of all who come in and out. I need you to get down there right now and stay until noon. Unmarked car, and wear a jumper over your uniform. Use this camera."

Bryce Rixon was not overjoyed. "What about the ten a.m. taskforce meeting?"

"You'll be back here by one o'clock and I will give you a full briefing then." And with that, Rixon left the office.

The business Tina had nominated had been under surveillance before. They suspected a small-time drug operation, no more. But it would suit her purpose today.

The team meeting was over by eleven o'clock. Inspector Sward couldn't make it, but the others were all there, including Graham James again.

Tina, Mike and Derek Sward had all agreed they could trust everyone in the room. They had to. Tina opened up, just leaving out details they did not need, like safe house locations and the senior 'Taskforce Cleanout' names. But she did lay out the full story on the massive shipment of drugs and arms plus the full details they had on the Moriarty mob.

Tina then said, "Jim Heggarty and now sadly Bryce Rixon are implicated with the mob. Heggarty is in a safe house under protection. He has given us a wealth of information. Bryce does not know we're on to him, so say nothing. I shouldn't have to tell you, but this is the biggest case any of us have ever been involved in and these vermin are cold-blooded killers. If anything leaks out of this room, we are all in the line of fire, and that includes our families.

"Later today, Mike will have a one-on-one with each of you. We have laid out leads to follow, tasks to do and your roles in the final operation. I suggest you work solo where possible to avoid putting others in harm's way. I can also tell you that I have cash on hand and the promise of whatever equipment and assistance we require. Just ask. Finally, we have four key people in witness protection but also one right in the mob's centre."

Tina went on to detail Anita, her role, her location and situation, plus her invaluable evidence. "So, if you hear 'Anita now' on your emergency channel and you are in the eastern suburbs, get there. ASAP. We do have a car nearby 24/7."

The meeting broke up and Tina went back to her office, shut the door and rang Derek Sward. She briefed him on this morning's meeting and the Rixon details and then said, "Derek, I need help," and sought his advice on how to handle the Rixon matter. "I need to bring it to a head very quickly."

They talked for a few minutes then hung up. Tina stiffened. She had never faced a situation like this. If she followed the inspector's advice, she would be condemning at least one fellow human being to almost certain death. This did not sit well with her. Tina was trying to weigh up the greater good versus the cost. It was a difficult decision. The inspector had said, "Tina, we are at war. We need to take out the enemy at all levels."

He was right, of course. There was a huge reward for society if they won 'the war'. This is what rank is all about, the big decisions. It is not a happy place, but someone has to do it.

Around one-thirty p.m., Tina summoned Bryce Rixon to her office. When he came in, he said, "This morning produced very little. There were a number of people going in and out. They all looked like regular clients. I have uploaded all the photos and they are ready for you. I don't think there was a meeting as such."

"Okay, send them through to Mike. Now I can tell you this. Our taskforce meeting today went well. I must give you the same warning I gave the others. This is the biggest challenge we have ever faced and you must not discuss this with a soul, not even the other taskforce members, until I am sure everything is okay."

Rixon nodded. Tina went on. "Last Friday at the Cobama gang raid we uncovered a close link to the Moriarty gang. Spider Kalowski, the head of the Calabro bikie gang from Redfern, was dealing in the SP room. We have threatened him with everything, including deportation and also passing on that he is collaborating with us. We gave him forty-eight hours to think it over. We know he is associated with the Moriarty gang as well and already have some of the names, and gained info when Jim Heggarty rolled over, but when Kalowski rang me on Saturday he spoke of a huge drug shipment about to arrive from Colombia for Moriarty. He has offered to tell us everything in return for protection and immunity. I've managed to clear that today and he is meeting me at five p.m. We should have him in a safe house by tonight. This is top secret."

Tina looked at Rixon. He sure was interested. "So, Bryce, I need you here tomorrow morning. Depending on what I get tonight, everyone will be given the full leads and information to follow up, and it is big. So, I want you to clear your desk and get ready to move at great speed tomorrow."

Rixon left quickly. He promised to be clear and ready in the morning. Fifteen minutes later, Mike came in and shut the door.

"He took the bait. He rang Moriarty direct," he almost whispered. "I've recorded it all."

"I almost feel sorry for Kalowski," Tina said. For the first time in her police career, she had knowledge of an impending felony but did nothing about it.

"We need a coffee," Tina said, and left to go and make it. She had a tight, knotted stomach but knew it had nothing to do with her treatment.

It was the longest hour that Tina could remember in her whole fifty-two years of life. She tried to concentrate on other matters, but it was impossible. At 3.04 p.m it all happened. Police radio went into top gear. Phones rang in almost every office. There was a huge event happening in Henderson Road, Redfern, near the railway yards.

There were reports of multiple gunfire, grenades and even a possible bomb blast. There were also reports of much bloodshed and a fire. It could be the Calabro bikie gang headquarters. Sirens were coming from all directions: police, fire and ambulance. Traffic had ground to a halt in the area, making it difficult for the first responders to get through. Redfern resembled a war zone. But back at Chatswood police headquarters, there was relative calm as Sergeant Bryce Rixon looked up and saw four detectives advancing on him, guns drawn. Blood drained from his face as Detective Sergeant Mike Broadfinger said flatly, "Bryce Rixon, you are under arrest," and then proceeded with the perfunctory legal advice on his rights.

Bryce Rixon remained silent, his shoulders slumped, as he was handcuffed and led to an interview room. Meanwhile, Tina picked up the phone and rang the commissioner first, and then Catie.

By the six p.m. news bulletins it was the lead story. Reports were coming in thick and fast of a major gunfight and multiple deaths, apparently a bikie gang warfare. There was fire damage to a whole block and, depending on which TV channel you were watching, it was supposedly linked to just about every major gangland crime over the past decade and beyond—even the Milperra massacre.

Tina felt her phone vibrate. She looked at the face. A single word from Derek Sward: "Bulls eye."

She put the phone back in her pocket as she strode towards the interview room to meet Bryce Rixon. The wonderful weekend down south was long forgotten.

Chapter Twenty-Four

The Qantaslink flight touched down in Canberra and the three nervous passengers disembarked with only hand luggage. Catie had spent the week putting together the best case she could. Brad and Bert were uptight. They realised this could have huge ramifications on the rest of their lives.

Catie had kept her editor, Bob Millman, in the loop. Their eleven-thirty appointment with the head of the Australian Defence Force, General David Ambleside, had been set up by Garth Peterson, who had also willingly provided the airfares.

Brad and Bert both had a great deal of respect for the general and had both met him at various medal and award presentations and military events over the years. They knew, deep down, this was the best thing they could do. They both had to get the monkey off their backs, no matter what the result and cost to them personally.

For General Ambleside, this was a most unusual meeting. In all the years he had known his close friend, Garth Peterson, this was the first time he had ever asked a favour, whereas the General had asked Garth on a number of occasions. He owed Garth—big time—but he was apprehensive, not knowing what it was all about. He liked to be on solid ground before any meeting. That was his style.

On the other hand, he remembered both of the SAS Commandos and their bomb disposal unit very well. Top men, both of them, the best the army had. Brad Spruce's Victoria Cross had been awarded for one of the bravest feats he had ever heard of. He wondered what could be so important. The general had read articles written by the journalist, Catie Lanyon, who was with them. He knew she was tops in her investigative field and he did not enjoy meeting journalists at any time. They normally spelt trouble.

Just after 11.25 a.m., the trio were ushered in to the general's office.

He had elected to have no staff on hand until he knew what it was all about.

The thirty-minute time allocation went way over. It was right on twelve-thirty p.m. by the time they shook hands and left the general's office. The trio silently headed for the Russell defence reception area to get a cab to the nearest café—ironically, the War Memorial Museum.

The general had slumped back into his seat and pressed the well-worn intercom button. "Andrea, get Ryan Fletcher and Amy McCabe in here now," he ordered tersely. Vice Admiral Fletcher and Air Vice Marshall McCabe needed to be in on this one really quickly. This was all about the fifth most senior officer in the Australian Army and did not auger well.

Catie had presented the case to General Ambleside. She left no stone unturned. She had not only Brad and Bert's statements, but also three other sworn affidavits about the Panwa massacre. Both Brad and Bert had then added their individual take on events.

Catie handed over the five sworn testimonies, plus copies of the boy's original reports from the sortie. The general had read them all as they talked.

He had asked why it had taken them so long to come forward and both lads responded as best they could. The general had picked up that both soldiers had been through tough times and it was obviously a mental health issue, as they were still both superbly fit.

Catie had then told the general that, as per the agreement she made weeks ago, she was presenting the whole case to the ADF twenty-four hours before it broke in the national media. The general didn't like that and said so, but knew they were lucky to get that. Normally the stories broke first and the ADF were on the back foot from the start, trying to minimise the damage.

Catie promised to ring him beforehand to be as cooperative as she could. General Ambleside was genuinely thankful. His parting words were, "Boys, I don't need this one little bit, but my respect for both of you has not diminished in any way. I am really sorry for what you have gone through. I will work to repair the damage in any way I can. Catie, I can't say it has been a pleasure, but tell my friend Garth no more favours, please. My heart can't stand it." He smiled, and they all parted on good terms.

The taxi dropped the trio at the War Memorial Café. They had not said one word during the short trip. Each was preoccupied, absorbing their own impressions of the meeting. They sat down and Brad quietly opened the conversation.

"Catie, I feel like a tonne weight has been lifted off my shoulders. Congratulations on that presentation. I am in awe how you pulled it all together so completely and so fast. Personally, I wish I'd done it years ago—with you on the team."

Bert echoed Brad's sentiments and asked, "How do you think he took it?"

Catie responded that she had been in many similar meetings over the years. "My first observation is that Garth was spot on. General Ambleside was the perfect choice to spill the beans to. He is obviously a decent human being and, I think, has a great deal of genuine respect for both of you. He realises what you have both been through but, I think it troubles him deeply that his beloved Defence Force is about to be savaged.

"The bottom line is that I think he is in your corner as he tries to work through this and that is a great start."

They talked over lunch, then ordered more tea and coffee until it was time to head to the airport for the return flight. Catie relaxed once the plane took off. She knew it had gone well. Her thoughts turned to Tina. Catie had only spoken briefly to her twice this week. The papers and TV/Radio news bulletins had been full of the Redfern massacre and Tina was also flat out on her major gangland challenge. Catie didn't know how Tina kept it up, especially with her health issues and treatment.

Catie, too, had her own challenges. She had told Bob Millman that she had one more major story to go in tomorrow before the nine p.m. deadline.

Bob couldn't believe Catie's sources were so productive. She had given him the heads up on the Redfern melee within minutes of it happening. The full story and accurate! Every other media outlet was speculating… he loved that.

Bob asked Catie about 'the big one' and she told him, "Soon, and you will be first to know." Bob was thankful but warned, "Catie, be very careful. We want a top flight journo on our team… not a dead legend."

Catie closed her eyes. She was looking forward to telling Garth how well it went when she saw him at treatment next Tuesday. She might even ring him earlier. She also thought General Ambleside might be able to help them with Jumalis' plight and another matter. Her mind was ticking over with all sorts of options.

CHAPTER TWENTY-FIVE

Bryce Rixon had tears rolling down his cheeks as Tina stepped into the room and shut the door. She turned on the video and recording gear, sat down, and said simply, "Why, Bryce?"

As the story unfolded, Tina began to feel sorry for him. After more than thirty years as a decent, honest cop Bryce realised his son, Marty, was hanging out with the wrong crowd. Despite a lifetime of good grounding, love and support from his mum and dad, and a rewarding eighteen-year career in Border Force, he would not listen to his dad's pleas and advice.

Just over eighteen months ago, Marty was caught and arrested during a botched armed robbery attempt at a twenty-four-hour service station. He was carrying his Border Force service pistol and it was his car they were using. To top it off, the boot was full of drugs, cash and stolen property. It had broken Bryce's heart. A life with so much potential, ruined.

Bryce had confided in his colleague, Detective Jim Heggarty, who came back to him an hour later saying his mate Pat Waldron was prepared to help and would be in touch. Two hours later, Marty was released from custody without charge. His name had completely disappeared off the police reports and charge sheet.

Bryce thought they did it out of respect for him. He knew it was wrong, but he desperately hoped it would be the wake-up call Marty needed. Bryce thought he could live with that. He had not told his wife, Prue.

But Bryce was dreaming. It wasn't long before Waldron was asking him for classified information—small things at first, then top secret files. He was hooked, and what was worse, Bryce saw his son was now driving flash cars and living a high lifestyle. Bryce realised Marty, too, was working for the mob on the waterfronts and airport, which explained his rapid Border Force promotions. It was all downhill for Sergeant Rixon from there, both as a dad and as a cop.

An hour later, before being led to the cells, Rixon signed a written interview report containing a lot of damaging information. He was offered bail but refused. He was ashamed. His life was over. Under Tina's instructions Mike went off to organise a safe cell for Bryce. He would need to be protected from the mob.

By the time Tina got back to her office, the first accurate reports had come in from Redfern. It appeared three carloads of hoods arrived at the Bikie HQ and began smashing their way in, and the bikies retaliated with gunfire. It was soon on for young and old. The whole thing was over in minutes. Grenades had been thrown, a fire broke out and two carloads of hoods escaped, but three of their mates and eight Colabro gang members were dead, including gang boss Spider Kalowski and his two senior lieutenants. There was no reason yet why the raid had taken place, but the car left at the scene was traced back to the Moriarty mob. It looked like a turf war.

The bikies clubhouse was reduced to rubble and both adjoining buildings were badly damaged by fire.

After Tina had rung Catie she hung up and was staring at the ceiling. She thought of Nick Pashilidis, and now another eleven were dead because of her actions. They all had mothers and fathers, brothers, sisters, children. Tina had had enough and had gone home before she completed the full report. It would have to wait until tomorrow.

Before leaving, Tina called Mike Broadfinger into her office and ordered him to arrest and charge Pat Waldron and keep him in protection. They would deal with him later.

Tuesday's chemo at the San was encouraging. Dr Emslie had the results of her scans and they revealed that the drugs were killing the shrinking cancer cells. "We are winning," the doctor said. "This is a positive sign, Tina. It means you can progress to immunotherapy after the chemo course is completed." The doctor went on to explain that immunotherapy is a biologic treatment using Tina's own immune system to fight the cancer.

Dr Emslie recommended an emerging treatment known as CAR T-cell therapy which would involve Tina's T cells being extracted and worked on in a laboratory so they can be used to attack whatever cancer cells were left in the body.

Tina was encouraged by the news but was feeling very flat and exhausted. She didn't know if it was today's chemo or yesterday's events. All she wanted to do was lay down and sleep. There would be no flower-power nursery lunch today. David drove her home and she was soon in bed.

Commissioner Palmer opened Wednesday's task force meeting by introducing Major Marc Andrews and Superintendent Dick Sellis. He then asked Tina to update everyone on recent events. It was a sobering narrative.

John Palmer congratulated her. "I know it has been a tough ride, Tina," he said, and then added more information that had come from Alan McDonald, Warren Hardcastle and Rusty Nolan.

"I must also add my sadness at the downfall of Sgt. Bryce Rixon. He was an excellent policeman and his entrapment by the mob is all too common today. Very sad," he said and looked at Tina. "Please keep him alive. He's a good man.

"So, we now have an amazingly accurate catalogue of explosive intelligence and our challenge is convert that into positive results. We have an opportunity here to smash one of the world's biggest cartels." He then formally introduced Major Andrews and Superintendent Sellis.

"Marc and Dick have been behind the planning of many of our high-profile busts and are experts at communications and intelligence gathering. They have convinced me to take the risk and allow the full shipment to be delivered right through to Sydney rather than remove and replace at Newcastle. We need to catch the key players, the top mobsters."

John Palmer then presided over an hour-long discussion to plan the sting. His white board and butcher's paper where kept very busy. The phones of some of Australia's unsuspecting top administrators and officials would be tapped and their computers hacked.

The meeting broke up with a great deal of expectation and excitement about the task ahead. The ship was on its way and due in

Newcastle in just ten days.

Tina drove back to Chatswood deep in thought. She would need to get Bryce Rixon bailed out and into a safe house. Somewhere no one would think of. She made a strong black coffee and went towards her office. She didn't make it.

Mike Broadfinger came around the corner. "Boss, I asked them to let me know as soon as you came in. Bring your coffee," he said, walking towards the main interview room. As they entered, Tina saw a handsome, fit young man staring at her with an almost pleading look in his eyes. He stood up as Mike introduced him.

"Chief Inspector Samuels, this is Marty Rixon, Bryce's son."

Tina quickly realised he was a totally devastated individual who had reached the bottom of the barrel and wanted to climb out. For all his failings, Marty had always loved his mum and dad. He realised early on that he was letting them down badly, but the temptation of all the trappings of the high life was too enticing. He was now deeply regretting this, and distraught.

Marty broke down a few times. He must have drunk six glasses of water during the forty minutes they were together. He admitted he had been weak.

What really impressed Tina and Mike was that Marty had thought out a feasible plan of redemption. He outlined his quick rise up the ladder in the Border Force operation, thanks to the mob connections. As a now senior officer, he was reporting directly to Shamus Moriarty and his key contacts worldwide, and other mobs as well. What he then offered Tina would put his own life on the line, but Marty just wanted to right the wrongs and come up in his parents estimation, no matter what the cost to him. It was all new intelligence, and big. He asked could he see his dad. Tina asked him to wait for a few minutes and went out with Mike. She returned alone five or so minutes later and sat down.

"Okay, Marty, we are going to give this our best shot. I hope you realise you are sticking your neck in a noose and there could be a fatal outcome." Marty nodded.

"First, it is not a good idea to see your dad right now for a number of reasons. He is totally devastated. What I can tell you is that

Commissioner Palmer himself contacted me earlier today to request that I do everything I can to help Bryce. He is still, despite everything, well-respected around here. Your dad has refused the bail offered, but I am going to convince him to take it and I will put both he and your mum into a safe spot. You will need to go back to your normal life and work with us.

"I just hope you weren't spotted arriving here. Mike is going to film and record your statement then take you down to our basement and drive you to North Sydney Station where you can catch a train. Not here at Chatswood. Too many eyes.

"I cannot emphasise enough the danger you are in. We will use your information on the arms shipment straight away, because that won't alert the Moriarty mob. They won't see the connection. Marty, whatever happens from here on in, your mum and dad will both be proud of you," Tina assured him.

Marty's shoulders rose as Mike walked in.

Tina left immediately to phone Alan MacDonald on his safe phone. Thankfully, he was still in Sydney and planned to fly back to Canberra on the last flight. Tina gave him all the new information, starting with the large Lebanese arms shipment about to leave Sydney plus details of two other shipments about to arrive in overseas ports. Alan cancelled his flight home to come directly to Chatswood.

"Hold Marty there till I arrive," he pleaded.

Chapter Twenty-Six

"**M**assive International Arms Trade Bust" screamed the front pages of all the World News Inc papers on Monday morning—an exclusive report by Catie Lanyon, Investigative Journalist.

It followed around the world on front pages for the next twenty-four hours. The story told about simultaneous raids yesterday at 1.45 p.m. eastern Australian time, 5.45 a.m. Libyan time and 6.45 a.m. Lebanon time in Sydney, Tripoli and Beirut. The raids had netted over thirteen-billion dollars-worth of illegal weapons and military equipment from guns, ammunition and grenades through to rocket launchers, submarine and aircraft parts from containers and warehouses worldwide. Even a tank had been seized.

It credited the Australian Federal Police Force as the mastermind, co-ordinating one of the biggest and most successful busts on the illegal arms trade in world history.

The massive shipments were headed for the pro-Syrian 'Hezbollah' Militia and the Lebanon Arms Bazaar. Reports were that a number of top officials had been arrested in all three countries.

The raids were timed to the split second so as not to alert the worldwide mobs and were carried out by Lebanese Armed Forces in Beirut and a garrison of the Libyan Army based in Tripoli, plus the Australian Federal Police under the personal direction of Deputy Commissioner Alan McDonald.

On the same day, the Sydney News Inc tabloids also broke another exclusive story—again by Catie Lanyon—on page five. "Senior Army General stands down—war crimes accusation". It reported that Major General Chris Ramsay, the officer in charge of Australia's top intelligence surveillance brigade and Australia's fifth highest ranking Army officer, had suddenly stood down. His resignation followed the emergence of reports about an operation six Uruzgan Provence in Afghanistan in 2012.

Seven unarmed civilians had allegedly been massacred in the town of Panwa during a major operation which had resulted in the capture of three senior Taliban recruiters.

The head of the ADF, General Ambleside, had issued a statement that information had recently come to light with accusations of a cover up. More details would be released soon. The story also included a paragraph on other alleged war crimes and reported that a former defence force media officer, Gerarde Page, had been arrested in Melbourne and charged with knowingly supplying false information to the media. Investigations into both matters were ongoing.

Editor Bob Millman rang Catie. "It looks like you're the only journo working the Redfern shoot out, the illegal arms trade and now war crimes. Catie, I don't know where all this is coming from, but please lie low. We are very worried about you," he said as he added his congratulations on an incredible few days.

"Don't worry chief. I'm in good hands," was Catie's response.

Catie had been surprised to get a phone call from Tina late Monday afternoon with the news that something big had happened. Tina gave her a detailed report on the Redfern shoot out. "All the others are speculating. You've got the real facts."

Certainly, her office welcomed the information and ran with it on the front page of Tuesday's News Inc metros. They loved it when it was fact and not speculation.

Then, Tina had phoned her again on Saturday. "This is your lucky week. You need to tell me where you will be on Sunday afternoon and have your pencil and paper ready. It's a big story and totally unrelated to our current case."

Tina was happy to be giving Catie these exclusive stories. She certainly appreciated all Catie had done to help her and was delighted to repay the favour. She also told Catie she would come up again next week to bring Catie and Alvaro up to date on a number of matters. "I will be bringing David. I would love it if he could meet you two plus Brad and Garth?"

"I think that will be fine. I will be seeing Garth at treatment on Tuesday, and Brad is coming up to Brisbane Thursday and Friday to follow up on his story," she said.

"Great. Try for Friday night and Catie, Alvaro and yourself must stay completely isolated. Anita tells us the mobs are going frantic and searching everywhere. David and I will make our own way from the airport to the hotel and I will liaise regarding the rest of the itinerary. David is really looking forward to meeting all of you."

In all her career, Catie had never felt so fulfilled. As excited and nervous as she was, she also felt a calmness. It was like she was in control—and winning. Juanita Nielsen would have very proud of her. Catie could feel her clapping from the grave.

Chapter Twenty-Seven

David Samuels couldn't believe his luck. Twice in two weeks he was sitting on the veranda of their holiday house on the waterfront at Mossy Point watching the mullet jumping on the ebb tide. But this time there was no Tina. Instead he had bought Bryce Rixon and his wife Prue. They had stopped in Batemans Bay to stock up with provisions to last for at least four weeks. David paid cash and kept the receipts, as instructed. "I will come down at least once a week to replenish milk, bread etc and to check all is okay."

The Rixons were both deeply grateful. Prue was having difficulty comprehending all these latest developments. Before David left, he gave Bryce a new phone and some contact numbers. He then called on both neighbours to advise them that his friends would be staying at the house for a few weeks. His parting words to the Rixons were, "Remember, walking, boating and fishing but no more. Sunglasses and hats at all times when outside. And no credit cards. Here is $1000 cash to get you through."

When Tina had entered Bryce's cell the day before, he had not wanted to talk to anyone. He just wanted to be left alone wallowing in his misery. Tina had spoken softly. "Bryce, you told me in the interview that you thought the armed hold up fiasco would be Marty's wake up call. Sadly, it wasn't, but your situation is. Marty is genuinely devastated that his actions have led to this and he is now helping me in a major way. You will be very proud of him, I know."

Bryce looked up, confused.

"But you are going to have to help him," Tina continued. "He needs to know you are safe. I want you to accept the bail offer. We have organised for Prue and yourself to go into a safe spot. You might even enjoy it."

David had been happy to do the chauffeur role.

Tina was putting out fires in all directions. Commissioner Palmer had called an emergency meeting on the Monday. Tina, Alan, Warren and Rusty had all been called in and Derek Sward had been asked to attend.

"Just for the record, I have never seen such a quick reaction to incoming new intelligence… and the success you lot pulled off, worldwide, over the weekend… It normally takes weeks, even months, to co-ordinate. Congratulations. I still cannot believe how efficient and effective it was, and the masterstroke of using the military in Lebanon and Libya instead of the police… Brilliant. Tina, you started it. What happened with Bryce's son?"

Tina explained how Marty was waiting for her when she returned from last Wednesday's Task Force meeting and how devastated he had been. She gave them a full account of all the information Marty had provided. "As Marty is now the mob's senior contact in Border Force, he had all the top-level intelligence. We've got it all on record. That's why I rang Alan and, fortunately, he was still in Sydney "

John Palmer then asked Alan to take up the story.

"Well," Alan started, "given the time differences between here and the Middle East, I did not get a wink of sleep for three days. My contacts were amazed at the details we had regarding all three ports. We had all the consignment details, container manifests and lading bills, plus warehouse/storage addresses at every point. They were able to mobilise the military forces instead of the police so the mobs were totally unaware we were coming. Especially in the Port of Beirut… You would not believe how much explosive material is stored there and the total lack of safety precautions. We have certainly earned some brownie points around the globe, particularly as we had all the mob contact details in all three areas."

Commissioner Palmer took over. "What a week. The Cobama mob, the Redfern massacre and now this… with the biggest challenge yet to come! The ship is still due in next week as planned."

He went on to explain that the Moriarty mob would be paranoid by now. All these things happening would be putting them on notice.

"They know we are aware that a shipment is coming. Bryce would have told them. That's probably why they have diverted to Newcastle. The good news is they think they took out the source before we got to hear all the details," said the commissioner. He then handed around the plans prepared by Dick Sellis and Marc Andrews. They were detailed, and would require a massive band of troops and equipment—drones, satellite imaging, extra CCTV cameras and standby choppers as well as all the ground troops, surveillance equipment and transport. A very thorough job.

"I want you all to take away these plans and advise me what personnel and equipment you can provide," said the commissioner. "We will be monitoring the ship's movements in case there are any changes, but at this stage all is on schedule. We will meet here again at ten a.m. Sunday for the final plan. I don't want to do a Zoom-type conference. Too many eyes and ears."

The meeting broke up and all headed back to their bases. Tina had called her team together at two p.m. and spent hours going over the plans in great detail, working out how they could best contribute.

Tina asked Mike to meet her in the office. "I am having chemo treatment all day tomorrow and will be in the office Thursday for a final run through. I'm then heading north for two days to see all our witnesses. Home Sunday. Can you cover me and stay in touch?"

"Sure thing, Boss, I reckon we're on top of this. Graham James is back on light duties next Monday, so I recommend we leave him here as our home base communications while we are all in surveillance or in Newcastle."

"Sounds good," said Tina. "I'm heading straight home as soon as I have booked flights and accommodation, and then I'll advise Catie."

There is a book titled *Famous Last Words*, and Tina's "I'm heading straight home" should have been a chapter. She had no sooner left the office and was heading along Lady Game Drive when her phone rang. It was Mike.

"Boss, you'd better get back to the office now. A couple of kids were canoeing on the Cooks River after school. They have just found Marty Rixon's bullet-riddled body floating in the reeds!"

It was a long night.

Chapter Twenty-Eight

Catie Lanyon could feel the tear running down her cheek. The doctor was trying to put a positive spin on her latest results with no success. The scans showed the cancer was spreading. "This is not too unusual at this early stage," she could hear the doctor saying. "Quite often the radiation takes a while to take." He kept talking.

But Catie was fearing the worst, she started thinking, *I've got to get this case with Tina completed while I can.*

She went into the radiation chamber feeling down. Catie knew nothing about Tina's latest challenge. News had not broken about Marty yet.

Tina was not faring much better. She had presented at the cancer clinic for round four of her chemo treatment the same morning, looking terrible. She had worked until four a.m. on the Marty Rixon murder. She was thinking, *that's now thirteen I've had killed—not my lucky number.* She had tried to sleep but kept thinking about Bryce and Prue Rixon.

Tina had wept silently, but David could feel her heaving. He turned on the bed lamp, got up and made a cuppa. They talked until daylight.

"Are you okay?" a receptionist had asked as she checked in to the clinic.

"Yep. I'll be fine, just a long night at work."

Her treatment finished by ten thirty a.m. David drove. They put on their favourite music, stopped at Braidwood Bakery around one-thirty for a quick bite, then drove straight to Mossy Point, arriving just after three.

Tina was feeling lousy from a mix of the chemo and the bad news she was about to give the Rixons. Tina realised they knew as soon as they saw Bryce and Prue. They were both in tears holding hands. The story had broken on the midday news, but Tina and David had not had the radio on.

"What happened," asked Bryce.

Tina told them everything right, from the moment Marty had come in to the station the previous Wednesday. "He was well aware of the risk he was taking and had spent twenty-four hours preparing the massive amount of critical information he gave us. It was all recorded, at his request, and was powerful. Thanks to Marty we've got them. Bryce, Marty was totally committed in wanting to redeem himself in your eyes for the damage he had done. Thanks solely to Marty, the world has just witnessed the demise of the largest illegal arms trading network that ever existed. He has exceeded beyond his highest expectation. You can both be very proud of him. We can only assume the mob figured out he was the only one who knew all the top-level detail and contacts. Either that or he was seen arriving at Chatswood."

Bryce looked at Prue. "What a mess. We can't change the past—neither Marty's or mine—but we can look to the future and work out a way to honour his memory. Thank God he went to you and the good guys."

The four of them talked for an hour or so, drank tea and coffee and devoured a huge apricot tart the Samuels had bought in Braidwood. At one stage, Bryce observed that the Moriarty mob might now be wondering if Marty gave police information on their current operation as well as the arms traders.

Tina replied, "Well, he did, but we already knew a great deal." She then explained the full story on the shipment due in Newcastle next week and their plans. "But you are right. They may now think we learnt something from Marty. We need to keep that in mind."

They also worked out that by delaying the funeral by a couple of weeks, the big case could all be over and Bryce and Prue could attend.

It was a sad day, but Tina was pleased they had gone down to see them. Though grieving badly, both Bryce and Prue were in a much better frame of mind as she and David drove out early that evening.

David was first to speak. "Well, you did it. Congratulations. They *are* now proud of Marty. Goal achieved." They drove on in silence, listening to more soft music.

Tina was due in the office next day.

Next morning, Tina received a call from the commissioner. "Is there any chance you could pop over to my office around eleven or eleven-thirty."

"Sure thing. I've got news on the Rixons I need to pass on," Tina replied. She arrived at his office just before eleven. Commissioner Palmer discussed Marty's murder and was pleased about Tina's trip to see the Rixons at Mossy Point. "You could not have found a better place for them to hide. Well done, and thanks for taking the time to give them some good news amongst all the bad. They really needed and deserved a lift."

The commissioner then handed Tina a bulky beige envelope. Tina smiled broadly as she saw the name and 'Tagar' on the envelope. Alvaro would be thrilled.

"I will deliver it in person on Friday. I am going to sit with both Catie and Alvaro to go over everything before the ship arrives on Wednesday. This will make his day—his year even."

John Palmer had advised that the planning for Olga's speaking tour was well advanced. "And she will be bringing both the children, but it's too early to tell Alvaro yet."

Tina was in a much better frame of mind when she got back to Chatswood HQ. She needed to arrange a task force meeting for tomorrow and go over last-minute details before she headed north. They had a lot at stake, and heaps more to do.

CHAPTER TWENTY-NINE

"**H**appy Anniversary!" David smiled and produced a small wrapped present, taking Tina by complete surprise. With everything going on, she had completely forgotten the date of their fifteenth wedding anniversary. Here they were, a stylish looking middle-aged couple, sipping coffee pool-side at the Marriott Resort Hotel in Surfers Paradise, having driven straight from the Gold Coast Airport to check in an hour ago. It was a salt water pool with a tiny sandy beach and colourful fish swimming around the sculptured artificial coral reef.

Tina was embarrassed as she opened the small velvet box to reveal a magnificent sparkling blue diamond pendant and silver chain. "I wanted a colour to reflect your mood," David chuckled, still smiling and feeling pleased with himself.

"Oh, David, this is *so* beautiful. I just don't know what to say, and I've got nothing. You'll just have to forgive me," she smiled back. "I'll wear it tonight as my new lucky charm."

They had both been in their mid-thirties when they met, fell instantly in love and married. Tina had already reached Sergeant and David had a successful design business.

It was late afternoon when they left the Marriott in an Uber. Catie had given Tina Garth's address with directions how to buzz for entry into the building and the lifts to the sub-penthouse. The Samuels arrived just before six-thirty and found themselves ushered to the lift and up thirty or so floors.

David was introduced to Garth and Meg as they made their way into the lounge area. What a place! What a view. What exquisite furnishings… even their own inbuilt horizon pool. Tina had never seen anything like it.

"The most expensive BBQ in Oz," laughed Garth. "Meg made me glass in both ends of the balcony to keep out the wind."

They chatted for a few minutes until the intercom buzzed announcing the arrival of the other three. Garth let them into the building then went to the door to greet them.

After introducing David to Catie, Alvaro and Brad they all sat watching the magic of the sun setting behind the Tambourine Mountains on the one side and, on the other, down over the masts of a historic tall ship sailing south past Broadbeach.

Later, Garth and Brad cooked. Meg laid out a delicious spread of salads, breads and dips and they all chattered and sipped away merrily as the twilight turned to darkness, revealing a million twinkling stars in the cloud-free night sky.

After a sumptuous feast, washed down with a few smooth Hunter Valley wines, Tina called for the floor. "I cannot remember the last time I felt this good. Wow. Thank you, Garth and Meg, for laying on such a magnificent repast. I so wanted David to meet you all, particularly with all the challenges we have faced together in the past and those still ahead.

"I feel it right that we should get to know each other. There is no better start than my introducing a person who, to me, epitomises everything that is good in this world of ours, and he also knows how hard it is to enjoy it. We know nothing about him. I give you Bernardo Rodriguez Sarmiento"

They looked at Tina quizzically until Alvaro stood up. He was surprised at hearing his real name.

"Alvaro," said Tina "You are amongst great friends who you can trust completely. Its time they heard about your journey to this wonderful evening, beginning with your school days in Bogota. Go for it my friend."

By the time Alvaro finished, half-an-hour later, you could hear a pin drop. He left nothing out. He told them about the murders, the mobs, the wiping out of most of his family, his escape and the dreadful refugee journey and his new identity. He talked of the much-loved family he had not seen or heard from for almost fourteen years, and the recent coded message in the Colombian paper that he read each week. He explained his five good years at the markets and spoke of his wonderful friend, Nick, who is now dead because of him. He talked of his dream to expose the evil mobs and bust them wide open, in both the country he now loves and the one he remembered from years ago.

Looking around the room as Alvaro spoke, Tina saw everyone listening intently as his life was laid bare.

Garth was the first to speak.

"Isn't it funny how each of us thinks life has been tough at times, and often challenging. Then you hear a story like yours, Alvaro. You have humbled me. It is a real privilege to be in your company," he said with feeling.

Tina spoke again. "Alvaro, I have a present for you." She handed him the beige envelope. As soon as Alvaro saw the word 'Tagar', tears welled in his eyes. He couldn't rip it open fast enough, like a kid with a Christmas present.

For a while everyone watched in silence at the joy written all over Alvaro's face as he poured over the photos and letters written by Olga, Rodriguez and Zarla. Eventually he looked into Tina's eyes and said simply, "This is the best day of my life. Thank you." He then proudly handed round the photos of his now grown-up family.

Tina thought to herself that regardless of the tough things she was dealing with at the moment, she was privileged to be in a position to give such unbridled happiness to a fellow human being.

Catie then stood up. "Firstly, I wish to propose a toast to Bernardo, his family and their future."

They all raised their glasses and drank

"Secondly, I, too, have had my eyes opened over the past few weeks, and that's a big admission from a journo. I am going to ask the only Victoria Cross recipient I know to enlighten us on his journey from West of Charleville to this unforgettable night. Take it away, Brad Spruce."

Everyone looked at Brad. The man-mountain was imposing when he stood up. None of them were aware of his Victoria Cross or, for that matter, anything about his SAS career.

He began hesitantly at first, but warmed to the task as he went along. He told of a young boy growing up on a 200,000-acre cattle station in outback Queensland. It was twenty-eight kilometres along a dirt track from the front gate and letter box to the homestead. He smiled at the memories of his late teens, when a big night out was a few beers at Roxanne's Fox Trap Roadhouse at Cooladdi—population three—about fifty kilometres south and the annual Adavale Rodeo and Camp draft. He described his college days at Toowoomba and being a proud cadet. He talked of his obsession with the Carnarvon Gorge, Mt. Moffat section area, the bushrangers, Mt Tabor's unbelievable Lost City, and the remarkable Bidjara mob around Augathella. Great people!

He went on to talk about his early days in the Army and transition into the elite SAS Commando Unit. Brad then described life on his three tours of Afghanistan, the huge challenges facing the Australian troops, and the events leading up to his Victoria Cross Award. He told of the bravery and loyalty of Afghan interpreters, like Jumali Qasan, and how concerned he was with his current plight.

He also talked in detail about the night he saw seven innocent, unarmed civilians murdered by a senior Aussie Officer, and the damage that had done to him and his mates over the years. He told how relieved they were now that the story is out in the open and the officer charged.

"I cannot thank Catie and Garth enough for making it come to fruition. Whatever happens from here on in is up to others. The burden is now off our shoulders."

There was a hush in the room. No one spoke for a minute or so.

Again, it was Garth who broke the ice. "I never thought I would say this, but the day I was diagnosed with cancer was my lucky day—no matter what the final outcome. My radiation treatment reconnected me to Catie and, as a direct link, resulted in Meg and I meeting all of you." He indicated the whole room. "I'm a lucky bloke."

He went on to tell them of his early work with Catie and exposing corrupt practices at the Wheat Board Corporation, and how he really enjoys the bad guys getting their just deserts.

"But what Catie has done over her career and what you have all achieved makes my success pale into insignificance. So, it's my turn to toast. To Brad, Bert, Catie and their future success with the ADF challenge. It was a pleasure for us to assist."

They all drank.

Catie took the floor straight away. "While we are all telling stories and comparing notes, I want to add that my own cancer diagnosis inadvertently put me back in touch with Tina when we met at Dr Emslie's. That has resulted in us all being here in this room. Sadly, my recent prognosis is not good, so I am just hoping to be able to see these current cases through." She gulped and went on. "My early reporting on a number of Tina's cases gave me a tremendous respect for both her ability and decency, so she was the natural 'go to' person when I needed help and protection recently. Best phone call I have ever made. So, I want to propose a toast to the finest law enforcement officer in the country. To Tina. May she forever prosper over the scum of this earth."

Tina accepted the toast with grace before she responded, "Life will always have its ups and downs, good people and bad, but for me, sometimes I wonder about my role. In the past few weeks, I alone have been responsible for the deaths of thirteen humans—some good, many bad—but all with loved ones. I don't think I can keep this up forever." She was obviously affected by it all.

Brad chimed in quickly. "Tina. I am in awe of the great work you do in making our world a better place and, if I may be so brazen, you are one of the lucky ones. You say you've lost thirteen people on your watch. You didn't pull the trigger. I did—a lot more than thirteen times. I also threw grenades, fired rockets and planted bombs. Sadly, a lot more than thirteen people died and many of them just like us, doing what they thought was right.

"It's what soldiers are trained to do, but that doesn't make you feel any better. It stays in your mind—every bloody bullet, every frozen face." Brad sat. Everyone nodded their understanding. It made an impact on the whole room.

Then Alvaro stood and almost admonished them. "Sorry, I not understand. I have been surrounded by killers, thieves and the evil drug cartels all my life. My family stood up for good and were murdered one by one. I would gladly give my life if I could make a better, safer world for my Olga, Rodriguez and Zarla. Yet, here I am, surrounded by good people doing good things, but could do so much more."

Every story has a turning point, and this was theirs. Everyone in the room looked at each other, then back to Alvaro, who went on, "At our two dinners you have spoken of bad police and politicians who destroy good. You all know magistrates who conveniently find errors in law that lead to many mobsters being acquitted on technical grounds, or who give them light sentences for horrible crimes. You all know of paedophile rings in high places, run by untouchables, and of clever killers and psychopaths roaming free because not enough proof can be found to convict them. You speak of known bikie gangs distributing deadly drugs. You also speak of your own cancers and other health issues. So, why not put your obvious skills together and take out some of these people while you still can. What have you got to lose?" He looked directly into the eyes of all.

After allowing that to sink in, Alvaro added, "And if you want me to pull the trigger, I will. I, too, have nothing to lose and would love to see a better world."

There was an eerie silence as that sank in. Eventually Tina spoke quietly. "Alvaro, your sentiments are noble. Yes—we would all like a better world, but we would need millions of dollars and we could hardly go out looking for sponsors, could we?" She smiled, trying to diffuse the tension.

Garth spoke up. "Why? That's where Meg and I come in. We've got the finances covered." Meg nodded in full agreement. Everyone was deep in thought.

After a moment of silence, Brad said, "Alvaro has touched on something we all dream of. A fairy tale where good triumphs over evil." He looked around at the others. "He's right, you know. We do know who those people are—the so-called untouchables. We do have, between us, the skills and ability to make a difference. I'm in, one hundred percent."

Unknowingly, they all found themselves looking at Tina, the law enforcement member of the group. Tina looked around the room before speaking in a very measured tone.

"I have been bought up and trained to respect the law, and I do. I realise we are not perfect and that sometimes the law is an ass. But we are streets ahead of most other countries and, by and large, live in a relatively stable and safe country." She paused. "However, deep down I would love to square the ledger for Nick Pashilidis, the Rixons and all those families destroyed by drugs and the mobs, and for all those kiddies whose lives have been ruined by those depraved sexual deviates. I am also sickened by those faceless politicians, crooked cops and judicial custodians who shield these vile creatures." Tina paused and looked at David. "With your blessing, my wonderful man, I'm in too."

David shook his head. He could hardly believe his ears. His righteous bride was 'talking dirty'. His eyes rolled. Slowly, he smiled and then nodded.

"Happy Anniversary," he said softly, and Tina grabbed her new diamond pendant.

Catie had watched all this unfold. She breathed in deeply and uttered two words: "It's unanimous," and then said as an aside, smiling, "provided I get the scoops."

The discussion that followed was animated and would be life changing for all of them. The risks and potential rewards were thrashed out at length. It was doable.

Around one a.m., Tina announced. "All I can say is that this was the last thing I thought tonight would produce. David and I need to go. We have an early plane to catch and we need a taxi back to the Marriott. You all know we have huge challenges coming up this week with the arrival of this massive drug shipment. I suggest we all get over that and reconvene to see if we all feel the same."

Everyone thanked Garth and Meg and headed out, all feeling melancholy.

Chapter Thirty

There was silence in the Leagues Club boardroom on Sunday morning as all involved in Taskforce Cleanout read and digested the reports and battle plans. Maritime reports had the ship still on time ETA off the coast Tuesday and docking around midday/early afternoon on Wednesday. Unloading should be completed within eight hours, as it was not a large ship.

Alan MacDonald had a thorough report on the movement of the three containers, with copies of all the paperwork pertaining to the wharf authorities and customs/border force agencies then onto the transporters. They even had the truck registration numbers.

Through his network, Rusty Nolan had procured the mobs' plans to receive, load, transport, store and then distribute over one billion dollars in drugs—deadly poison for millions of addicts on the eastern seaboard—plus arms and other material.

Dick Sellis and Marc Andrews had turned a logistical nightmare into a formidable battle plan with many backup scenarios.

Inspector Palmer congratulated them. "All up, there are over eight-hundred men and women involved from our side, as there are many locations to be raided simultaneously in Sydney, Melbourne, Canberra and Brisbane. We propose to slowly drip-feed everyone into their various positions, starting Wednesday morning in Newcastle. Hopefully they will all be in position at the wharves by just on dark. The others will be called, depending on the truck departures with the three containers. We envisage they will be cleared by the port authorities no earlier than eight p.m.

"Normal practice would see the full ships' cargo cleared from the wharves by midday Thursday, so we could be in for a long night. We are making provisions for forty-eight hours—just in case.

"The weather forecast is not pleasant: rain, wind and possible mild storms from mid-afternoon Wednesday, then clearing Thursday morning. Nothing too dramatic."

They talked on through a light lunch in the room, and broke up just after two p.m.

"Good luck, everyone. We can only hope we have covered all the bases, and we get a good result. I suggest, if possible, you relax as much as possible over the next thirty-six hours. I know that is not easy for some of you. I am now handing over the reins to Dick Sellis and Marc Andrews to conduct the operation in Australia, and Alan MacDonald to do the same in Colombia. All contact will now be through them," he concluded.

With that they mingled for a few minutes before heading out.

"Any word from the Rixons?" the commissioner asked Tina as they were heading out through the door.

"David is down there with them as we speak. I will know more, later tonight."

"Okay. I hope your treatment goes well on Tuesday."

As soon as she got to Chatswood HQ on Monday morning, Tina called her team together and circulated the full report to everyone involved. "Remember the golden rule: expect the unexpected," she told them, "and keep your radio use to a minimum, using only coded messages."

After the meeting broke up, Tina and Mike sat, going through everyone's role 'just in case'. They checked to see if they had missed anything. Tina was worried about Anita Collins and how they were going to get her out as the operation got underway. She was also concerned about all those in 'safe' houses.

"We seem to have people hidden from Southern NSW all the way up to Queensland. Thankfully, only Heggarty and Waldron need 24/7 security. I just hope word doesn't get out as to where they all are," Tina said to Mike.

The bulk of Tina's team would be in and around Sydney. At Newcastle, there were enough to monitor the truck movements in and out of the wharf precinct at both the entry and exit gates. Plus, there were sporadic units in place along the motorway to Sydney. The real test would be to co-ordinate the simultaneous planned raids to warehouses, offices, homes and bikie clubs all over the country and in Colombia.

Tina decided to place herself at Parramatta HQ with Inspector Sward. They would co-ordinate raids at the delivery point. The markets were only ten minutes away. On arrival, just after six p.m. on Wednesday evening, she was welcomed by Derek Sward and taken straight into the Operations/Communications Centre where she settled in for the night ahead.

Confirmation had come through just after three p.m. that the TSMV Kotravik, registered in Panama, was secure at the wharf. A few hours later, the arrival of the three containers on the dock was reported. The weather bureau had understated the conditions. It was bucketing down, windy, and lightning was forking eerily across the dark sky. Just on 9.45 p.m., the first truck arrived, then the second before midnight. The third rig arrived around 1.15 a.m. There were a few nervous concerns that the earlier trucks had not come to the exit gate.

At precisely 2.24 a.m., things took a turn for the worse. As part of Dick Sellis's backup plan, he had a man stationed at the heavy vehicle weighbridge near Wyong. That man reported that one of the mob's trucks had just pulled in and was being weighed. Panic stations!

Back at the wharves, two men were immediately dispatched to check out the containers. It was still pouring rain and visibility with binoculars was not easy through the perimeter fence.

"Two birds have flown!" The call resonated over the radio. The message was loud and clear. All of a sudden, the taskforce team galvanised into action. Two containers were missing, but no trucks had been seen exiting. Dick Ellis then pressed the 'go' button for all the Sydney, Melbourne and Brisbane teams to get into position.

Within ten minutes, they had established that a rarely used exit to the rutile plant at the back of the precinct had been used that night. There were fresh tyre marks evident. Around 2.45 a.m., they witnessed the third truck exiting the same gate and heading down the dirt track.

Dick Sellis advised all units to stay out of sight. Two new units were quickly placed just south of the weighbridge, and one of the Newcastle units was shadowing the last container as they drove south through

Hexham, towards Sydney.

Inspector Sellis was concerned. They had no idea where the third container was. He crossed his fingers. The registration number of the truck at Wyong weighbridge proved it was the second truck to enter the wharves. Where was the first?

By five a.m., the truck from Wyong was arriving on Sydney's outskirts, where it was still raining, and onto Pennant Hills Road with shadows in tow. About an hour later, the next truck was being weighed at Wyong—but still no sign of the missing container.

This was not how it was supposed to happen. Sellis told those near the markets to report the truck's arrival but take no further action until all three trucks were located.

By six a.m., Superintendent Sellis was worried. The first truck was now in the market's warehouse and the second nearly there. In fact, it, too, arrived at the warehouse just after 6.15 a.m.

"Hold your positions." The call went out to everyone. Ellis knew he couldn't hold on for long, but he didn't want to lose millions of dollars-worth of drugs.

It was nearly seven a.m. when his prayers were answered. A report came in from the agent placed at Chinderah weighbridge, just south of the Queensland border. The first truck was being weighed. Sellis thanked his lucky stars.

An urgent call to Tweed Heads Police had an unmarked vehicle following as the truck left the weighbridge heading north. Dick Sellis breathed a sigh of relief. Within five minutes, he had alerted the Brisbane stake out team already in position near the mob's known warehouse on Howard Smith Drive at the Port of Brisbane that the container was on approach to them. The mob shared the complex with one of Queensland's most notorious bikie gangs, The Grinches.

Sellis estimated that the ETA would be just over an hour away and advised every other unit around the globe to prepare for the raid around that time. The Sydney Market's team were getting edgy and reporting the arrival of a number of smaller enclosed tray-back trucks and motorcycles at the warehouse.

At 8.21 a.m. Sydney-time, an urgent message: "Go, go, go" went out to every unit worldwide. This was it. The Brisbane team had reported, a few minutes earlier, that the container had arrived and was being backed into the warehouse. It seemed as if every single unit involved in Australia had instantly galvanised into action around the nation. Tina had stayed in the Parramatta HQ to co-ordinate things at the markets as Inspector Sward was with the team on site. Once Tina was sure everything was moving and under control, she honoured her promise and rang Catie.

The Brisbane raid was noisy and fast. Sirens, cars with blue and red lights flashing, police and dogs swarmed into the warehouse. The truckie had just switched off his engine and there were only half-a-dozen people around the dock area. The bosses were upstairs in the office and taken by complete surprise. They offered little resistance. At the same time, the police raided the bikie gang HQ next door and arrested five sleepy 'Grinches' before they searched the premises and struck the jackpot.

Not so in Sydney. The Moriarty Mob's warehouse was surrounded and undercover police were in place throughout the markets themselves. Carlos Carezo and Dave Gillespie had no time to react. They were on the floor and handcuffed in seconds as other police went around the stands systematically arresting a number of people on various stalls.

But things were different at the mob's warehouse itself. The Initial shock wave of troops with guns drawn, dogs and handlers had the desired effect on those in the dock area and around the trucks. Most hit the floor immediately on the yelled command over the police megaphone.

From somewhere up above, an automatic burst of gunfire caused pandemonium. The whole place erupted. At least two police were killed and return fire came from everywhere.

Some of the mob saw it as a chance to run for it, but the dogs soon had them collared. Others drew guns in the hope of escape. None did. Some were hit, and the rest soon threw down their weapons and knelt.

A number of those upstairs died in the hail of gunfire. Others, including Moriarty himself, had been hit but were still alive. Many of his henchmen had not fared that well. Sirens kept coming: ambulances, more police, even the Fire Brigade. The markets were evacuated quickly. No one had to be asked twice as the gunfire rang out. They fairly bolted.

In cities around the world many similar stories would be told.

There is no doubt the surprise element worked a treat. There were arrests amongst senior political and Justice Department figures, even senior police at a number of stations in Sydney, Melbourne, Brisbane and Canberra. Border Force were not immune, and several gang members were killed or injured at a number of Bikie Gang Headquarters in three states.

Many shady lawyers, barristers and Queen's Counsellors were about to become even wealthier.

Tina was listening on the police radio to all the reports filtering through. One was from Melbourne Airport, where a Border Force officer had been killed in a motorcycle accident trying to evade arrest. Her ears pricked up. There was a report about gunfire "just off Botany Road at Mascot, policeman down".

Christ, that must be Heggarty, she thought. *The mob must have found him.* But before she had time to blink, Tina froze.

"Attention all units. Bondi area. Multiple gunshots and explosions. Police Operation. Home Unit block, Corner of Birrell Street and Park Parade."

Tina felt weak. Tony Morabito's—and they hadn't got Anita out yet!

"Oh, God—Anita," she gasped. "Please no. Please no."

Georgia McHenry was nearby and heard Tina. She rushed over "Chief, are you alright?"

Tina wasn't. It was all too much.

Georgia was worried about Tina. Mike had confided in her about some serious health issues. The three of them were very close. She went to grab coffee from the nearby canteen.

Tina sat wringing her hands, ears glued to the radio, trying to work out what was happening at Bondi. Her phone rang. It was Mike. "Bad news, Boss. Don't know the full story yet, but Jim Heggarty has escaped. He somehow got the gun from his escort, killed him and got away. I'm on the way there now. I'll call you as soon as I have anything concrete."

Tina blinked. "Thanks Mike. Keep onto it," was her automatic response. She told him about Bondi. *Bloody Heggarty—he'll keep,* she said to herself as she rang Dick Sellis.

"Sorry Dick, I know how frantic things are, but I need to know what's happening at Bondi. Anita is in that unit. It's Tony Morabito's."

"Okay, Tina. I'll get onto it now," said Dick and hung up. Tina and Georgia tried small talk while listening to the police radio. It didn't work. They were too edgy. Eight minutes went by—an eternity.

Tina's phone buzzed. She saw it was Inspector Sellis. "Hi, Dick. How'd you go?"

Tina listened. Her heart sank. Tears were rolling down her face. Georgia could see it was horrible news and feared the worst.

Dick reported that their team had raided the unit as part of the original plan. Morabito and others were home and started shooting. Police fired tear gas and grenades into the unit and went in firing. All five people in the unit had been killed. There had been no official identification yet. "But it appears Wipeout Morabito and his girlfriend were two of those killed," Ellis finished.

Tina felt sick "But Dick, There was a one-year-old little girl in that unit!"

"Oh shit. There is no word on that. Let me get back to those on the ground." He hung up.

Tina was totally flat. She drained the dregs of her coffee and picked up the phone to ring Catie. She was dreading the call.

CHAPTER THIRTY-ONE

As arranged, after Tina's phone call to report everything was on schedule, Catie had gone, on Thursday morning, to Alvaro's for breakfast on the balcony. Catie thought both of them could do with the company.

Tina had given her just enough details of the plans for Catie to be able to make sense of all the news when it began filtering in from around the globe. Catie was amazed at the scope of the exercise. She had phoned both Garth and Brad telling them to stay tuned to the TV news channels from breakfast tomorrow as Tina and Alvaro's big case was about to come to a climax.

"You should see the results of a lot of hard work and heartache," she told them. Garth told Catie he may soon have some news on Brad and Bert's hopes to keep Jumali in the country. "Early days, but we do have some people in place. It will probably take another trip to Canberra," he had said.

Catie thought that was potentially good tidings. She then rang her editor, Bob Millman, and gave him the outline story and Bob became quite excited. He responded, "Wow, we are going to need all hands on deck sometime early tomorrow. Okay. We'll be ready."

Catie was hoping everything would go well. This was the original deal and much bigger than she had anticipated.

When Tina's call came through just after 8.30 a.m. next morning, Catie listened and took lots of notes. Tina had to go, but promised to ring back as soon as more details came in. Catie rang Bob Millman and unloaded all the details. Bob immediately went to work.

Catie and Alvaro didn't have long to wait.

"Breaking News. Breaking News," flashed across the screen, telling of gunfire and explosions breaking out around Sydney markets. That was quickly followed by the mayhem spreading to Bondi, near Waverley Park and Mascot, and there were reports of a number of raids all over the city. A major international police operation was underway.

Within minutes, just about every TV network, radio station and on-line media outlet was reporting on simultaneous raids occurring all round Australia and Colombia. The story was becoming bigger by the minute.

About fifteen minutes after her first report from Tina, Catie's phone lit up. She looked at the face. "Hi, Tina." Catie was smiling. "Wow. You sure have started something."

Alvaro watched her as the colour drained from her face and she collapsed into her chair. "No, no, please no! Not Anita," was all he heard. She began sobbing uncontrollably.

CHAPTER THIRTY-TWO

"**O**ur Planet Saved" was the front-page headline of *The New York Times*. An exaggeration, yes, but all the world's media were reporting similar stories of a massive upheaval in organised crime investigations. Hundreds of arrests—top politicians, bureaucrats, top police and senior judiciary members along with drug lords. They also reported multiple deaths and injuries occurring during the raids, some in the various police forces, military troops and border force organisations.

There was no doubt the world would be a better and safer place following this major successful Operation Cleanout. Over seven billion dollars-worth of drugs had been recovered, along with an enormous cache of arms, cash, ammunition and stolen goods.

Promoters and event/show organisers all over the globe were furious. They could not get any space in either the electronic, print or social media to push their special events, concerts, shows or sporting events. It was all about this massive crime busting operation.

For the second time in two weeks, Australia was given the credit of leading, uncovering and co-ordinating a global operation that dismantled more of the world's major organised criminal organisation networks.

Tina hardly surfaced for the next ten days. Life was full of ups and downs, debriefings, media scrums and reports. Many of her team were recommended for all sorts of awards and accolades.

The major high for her had been the call from Alan MacDonald to say they had located Anita's eighteen-month-old daughter safe and well. It appears Anita had run into a neighbour's apartment asking them to mind her. Tina had immediately rung Catie with the good news and had called every day since, just to make sure they were okay.

The saving grace for Catie was that there was so much news—so many breaking stories—it kept her mind off Anita to some degree. She had taken the death very badly.

Bob Millman and his team at World News Inc were run ragged. They were lucky to get four hours sleep a day.

Catie reported that Alvaro was in high spirits. He was overjoyed with the operation's success—particularly in Colombia—and his part in it. He had read and re-read Olga and the children's letters many times. Life was certainly improving.

Catie also reported Alvaro had decided to let his hair grow back to its natural dark colour.

"I talked him into staying clean shaven. He looks much better. But his hair now looks like a rugby league player... blond top and dark roots. It looks hilarious. She also confided to Tina that she was now the 'blue-eyed girl' at work.

Tina had promised to come up as soon as she could. "Maybe we could visit Anita's mum."

"That would be so great," Catie replied. "I'll hold you to it."

David had headed south to be with the Rixons at Mossy Point during the operation, as moral support for both of them. He decided to stay on for a few days, as Tina wouldn't be home much. Their neighbours had all seen Tina on the news broadcasts and were inquisitive. The Rixons were extra pleased to have company and they all followed the events of the operation with great interest.

Garth, Meg and the Spruces had also been following the news in awe. Brad had been pleased to get news from Catie that they were on Jumalis' case and making some progress. He so wanted to repay Jumali for his huge risks and loyalty over the years.

Both Brad and Bert had been called to give evidence before the panel investigating possible war crimes. They both thought it was fair but were apprehensive about the final outcome in respect of their own actions and cover-ups years before. They later heard the major general had been officially charged.

Tina was a mini celebrity at her cancer clinic on the Tuesday, as most had seen her on many TV interviews and news reports. Dr Emslie reminded her she was still only two-thirds of the way through the chemo course.

"We won't know the outcome until the end, but there's little doubt that your adrenalin rushes would be pushing the medicine through your veins at great speed, and that is good," the doctor had said.

Tina received an email from Commissioner Palmer asking her to attend a police luncheon at Day Street Headquarters on Friday. She emailed back her acceptance.

As Tina was arriving at Day Street, she was greeted and congratulated by a number of her colleagues on a job well done. Tina was just hoping she was looking okay, as the treatment was starting to take its toll. She was tiring quickly as the mad rush was slowing down.

There were around two dozen of her senior colleagues in the room, and Tina was glad to see Inspector Derek Sward and Deputy Commissioners Alan MacDonald and Warren Ambleside were all there as she hadn't seen any of them in person since the operation itself. She sat next to Derek and the lunch proceeded with a real buzz in the room. Tina was not surprised that Rusty was missing.

Commissioner Palmer called for order after the main course was cleared.

"I don't have to tell anyone in this room that events over the past month have lifted both our NSW and Federal Police morale and reputation to an all-time high. You are all to be congratulated for the role you played in it.

"We have demonstrated teamwork straight out of the text book and led by example. Australia is very proud of you, and so am I.

"This lunch is a chance for me to say a personal thanks to each and every one of you and ask you to please take that back to your own teams and pass it on," the commissioner continued. "Sadly, we have lost a few good people as a result of the operation, and I have kept in touch personally with each of the families involved. Any loss is tragic. I do encourage each of you to attend as many of the fallen police funerals as possible. People keep telling us that this is part of the job. I don't think they understand the hurt or the loss. We will miss them," lamented the commissioner.

"It is always dangerous to single out one officer when so many have done so much but, today, I want to propose a toast to Superintendent

Tina Samuels. Yes. That's right. Superintendent Samuels was officially promoted at noon today," he finished, beaming at Tina's stunned surprise.

The room erupted into spontaneous and prolonged applause. Tina just sat and blushed. "Expect the unexpected," she had told her troops just a few days ago. Her new badges of rank were handed to her by Deputy Commissioner Kel Mackay. "Well done. I can't wait to hear how you've achieved it," he said.

As soon as she got back to the car, she rang David and then headed back to Chatswood HQ.

Chapter Thirty-Three

The prosecuting sergeant was presenting his case to the panel of two senior police officers and an independent appointment who was a Family Court Magistrate. These were normal police protocols. Perception of independence was everything.

Tina had received the call midweek to advise the hearing had been set and that Bryce Rixon was required to be there.

Tina was nervous on two counts. This could alert the mob that was left as to Bryce's whereabouts before their trials, and also did not give Bryce much time to prepare his defence.

She had phoned Mossy Point and Bryce said he wanted to get it over and done with ASAP and was happy to go with the Monday. He was quite prepared to pay whatever price the enquiry deemed necessary for his wrongdoings. He understood the system all too well. He knew he would more than likely go to gaol and was only worried about Prue. Tina had assured him that Prue would receive lots of ongoing support, including hers. Tina had organised for David to pick Bryce up early and for him to be dropped at a prearranged spot to transfer into an unmarked police vehicle with an escort for transfer to Day Street HQ and arrive just before nine-thirty a.m.

Bryce was charged on three counts, the most serious being the passing of classified police information to criminal gangs, a major crime in the eyes of the law. Bryce immediately pleaded guilty to all three charges so that it would be over fairly quickly.

Tina was pleased that the prosecutor had presented a credible case without overdoing the dramatics. Bryce's counsel was a well-known and respected defence attorney. She put Bryce on the stand and led him through all the events and circumstances leading up to the wrong doings.

Bryce was stoic, breaking down only once, and that was when

the death of his son, Marty, was mentioned. When Bryce was stood down the attorney called only two character witnesses, Tina and the commissioner himself.

The panel reserved their decision and Bryce was led out from the courtroom and taken back to the basement.

The same plain-clothes police car and escort vehicle left the building some five minutes later and they appeared not to notice the dark SUV that pulled out behind them. It began following the police as they drove south out of the city, all the way, nonstop, to Parramatta Police HQ, where both cars pulled up out front and everyone got out. Bryce Rixon was not among them.

Back at Day Street, no one had noticed the light grey delivery van and driver that had exited the car park around twenty minutes after the earlier police convoy. Bryce was safely driven back to Mossy Point by David after their city rendezvous.

Tina and the commissioner had a quick coffee in the police canteen. They both agreed that Bryce had received a fair hearing. Tina advised him she was having more treatment tomorrow and would finalise all her reports by Friday, as she was the taking next week off.

The commissioner thought that a great idea but warned, "Keep watching your back Tina. I've a feeling this is not over yet. It will take months to get all these cases to proceed and we need to be vigilant as the stakes are high."

He finished off with the fact that they had no leads at all on Jim Heggarty, but would leave no stone unturned.

Chapter Thirty-Four

The mood in the barbecue houseboat was quite subdued. All six passengers were mulling over the last hour's discussion, letting it all sink in. Tina had flown in the night before under an assumed name. Brad had driven down from Brisbane with his SAS Commando mate, Bert Hunter. "Bert knows everything going on. We are in this together," Brad had told them. Everyone was totally okay with that. Alvaro and Tina had driven to Tweed Heads wharf with Catie. Garth was already there. He had arrived a bit early to finalise his booking and load the food, beverages and some fishing gear onto the boat.

Alvaro produced a picnic basket. Lifting the gingham cloth, he revealed some delicious iced treats. "Bogota cup cakes. I bake them just for you. My grandmothers recipe," said the beaming Colombian.

After the obligatory safety talk by the houseboat staff, they cruised west along the Tweed River towards the picturesque Rous River, with Brad at the controls.

There was much discussion around the success of the mob operation both in Australia and Colombia. Tina pointed out they still had a long way to go to get all the convictions. The discussion then went on to who and what would be standing in the way of justice. They talked about corrupt witnesses, sympathetic magistrates, gang lawyers, false testimonies plus the challenges close to home, the protection of Alvaro, Catie and Bryce.

Police in both countries had a mountain of crucial evidence supplied by these three, plus those ex mobsters who had turned states' evidence on a plea deal. A number of them had already been put in safe houses. This included some of the high-profile people caught up in the arrests, including the Australian Federal Minister for Immigration, Senator Garry Poplas, who quickly decided to come clean when he realised he was staring down the barrel of a life sentence. He would bring down many others.

Police also had the recorded and filmed evidence of Marty Rixon and Jim Heggarty. The commissioner had said both were admissible evidence in court.

Over a sumptuous barbecue with some of Meg's delicious salads and fresh, crusty bread rolls they talked about Anita, Nick and the many good people killed trying to bring these people to justice. They talked about vicious gangs of thugs seeking power, territory and illegal wealth. They went back as far as Juanita Neilsen, Alvaro's family and so many others. It had been going on for a long time. In between, they did some fishing in the Rous River, looking up at the majestic Mt Warning, with Alvaro proving to be an expert..

Catie had then said with steely resolve, "Our cause has been strengthened by the death of Anita. I feel responsible and I am really keen to see us bond into a formidable group and take these bastards out. Are we all still in?"

They all instantly reaffirmed their stance. Alvaro even reminded them, "Remember, being a foreigner, I am more than willing to pull the trigger where necessary to take out some of these evil human beings. After all, I will be dead within hours if they find me first. This is war."

The team began to take shape and listed some of the possible priorities as well as the challenges.

Brad had pointed out there was still the possibility that he and Bert could face prison as a result of the war crimes hearings and Catie reminded them that she, Tina and Garth still had major health issues, so time was of the essence. Alvaro chimed in, "I may be taken out before any of you if my real identity comes out."

Before docking, they had agreed on some short-term goals. One was to keep working for Jumali Qasan and his family to stay in Australia. Garth had reported a hurdle here. A senior immigration officer was resolute on his recommendation for deportation to Afghanistan. "There is something sinister here," Garth said. "His last four deportations have all disappeared into thin air soon after their returns. Their families are beside themselves. There is something amiss and people are looking into it."

Another was Tina's desire to find Jim Heggarty. "We've got all the evidence recorded on film and I would love to see him taken out and made to pay for my colleagues."

Alvaro had started the discussion on the names of those evil "untouchables." They had plenty to pick from. After a lively discussion, they chose a shortlist.

As they were unloading their gear everyone thanked Garth and agreed to talk again in a few days, after following up on the tasks set for each of them.

Next morning, as soon as Catie's radiation was completed, she and Tina drove to Brisbane where Anita's mum was expecting them. They were pleasantly surprised to find Anita's little girl with her nan. She sure was a cutie. "Just like mum," Catie said.

Vera Collins was in her early sixties, widowed and living in a small duplex bungalow in Mt Gravatt. She had baked scones which the girls smelt as soon as they walked in. As expected, she was devastated at the loss of her much loved, only daughter. "I just can't work out why she ended up with such awful people. She was such a funny, happy and loving child. A bit of a tomboy, for sure, but she loved her cuddles and hugs," she remembered. "Her brother, Max, is a minister and will officiate at her funeral."

Both Tina and Catie had expressed their respect and admiration for Anita and told Mrs Collins how she had done so much good bringing the mob down, even knowing the risks. "She was a brave, decent girl" Tina said.

"Was she working for you and the other police?" Mrs Collins asked.

"In a way, you could say that," replied Tina.

This made Anita's mum feel a bit better. "Then that explains why she asked me to give you this Catie," said Vera Collins producing a small package. "When she was here two weeks ago, she told me if anything happened to her I was to get this to you."

Catie opened the small package which revealed two USB sticks. They thanked Mrs Collins and assured her they were sure this would really help the police in their efforts to dismantle the gang.

They both offered ongoing help with Anita's little girl and said they expected to be at Anita's funeral on Friday, if possible.

Back at Catie's they inserted the USB stick, sat back and watched. Forty or so minutes later they looked at each other. Catie simply said, "Shit."

Tina was reeling. "How could she have possibly filmed those clips without being caught? How brave was that! My God, it's not often I'm stuck for words."

Anita had given them 'Mr Big' on a platter, and neither of the girls had seen that coming. Joe Iminez was a well-known, multiple night club owner and developer/businessman from the Cross. He had been investigated many times, but nothing ever stuck, and he had never been indicted. Yet, here he was giving direct orders to Moriarty. Explosive, incriminating stuff, but what threw Tina was the third person in the room. Catie hadn't recognised him but Tina sure had. She was livid.

Catie said, "I've been trying to get something on Iminez for years, as have many others, but he always covered his tracks. Wow, we've got the bastard now—and how," she said. "This calls for a glass of red and a toast to Anita." Later they headed out to pick up their ordered pizzas and on to see Alvaro.

On Wednesday morning, Tina went into Surfers Paradise and bought two new phones and two $100 prepaid sim cards for cash, giving bogus names and contact details for both. She needed to make a number of important calls and did not want them traced back to her own phone. The other one was for Catie.

Tina had a problem. She so wanted to relax and spend the rest of the week here, and also to go to Anita's funeral in three days. But she also had lots to do and really needed to be in Sydney—and quickly. All this was immediately sorted as she was driving to meet Catie. Tina's phone rang. It was Mike.

"Sorry, Chief. Tried not to ring but all hell has broken out here. They have found Waldron's safe house. All three are dead—the two police guards and Waldron himself. I'm on my way over there now."

"Bloody hell, Mike. How did they find out? Crap! Okay. I'll get back tonight. I'll give you a time when I get my flights." Problem solved.

Tina rang Catie, then drove straight to her apartment, packed and checked out. She had been able to get a flight leaving in two hours. Catie was already at the airport when Tina arrived. After an automatic check-in, they went for coffee. Catie gave Tina two extra USBs of Anita's crucial evidence.

"I ran off five extras and will put the others with my sealed envelopes."

They talked about their new mission and also Catie's failing health. Tina was really starting to worry about Catie. She gave her the new phone and promised to call daily. "Anytime you need to call someone without a trace, use this one, and stay out of sight."

The flight left on time. Tina settled in. All she could think about was Anita's revelations and the third man in the room—Deputy Police Commissioner Kel Mackay.

Chapter Thirty-Five

"After taking into consideration all the circumstances in this case including over thirty-five years of exemplary service, the loss of his son and the contribution of both father and son to recent major successful police operations, this panel is aware that Bryce Rixon has tendered his resignation from the NSW Police Service and we propose no further action to be taken and no conviction recorded. Case closed."

These were the words of the panel chair at the Day Street HQ hearing on the Tuesday after the October long weekend. Bryce Rixon was not there, but Tina was, and she beamed as she left the room to phone Mossy Point on her unregistered mobile phone.

"Bryce, this means you have a future not tarnished with any baggage." Tina told him "After all this is over, you have a clean slate."

Bryce was certainly happy with the result, but reflected sombrely on the events leading up to it. There was no cause for a celebration, but there was hope for the future and the chance to rebuild his life. Both Bryce and Prue were extremely grateful.

The past month or so had been a challenge for Tina, wearing two hats: her police duties and her new team activities. Lots of things had been happening; lots of ups and downs. She was wrestling with internal demons.

Leaving Bryce's hearing she had been driven straight to the San Hospital Cancer Clinic for her final chemotherapy treatment. Tina was hopeful that next month's scans would deliver some good news. She was certainly confident and all the signs were good. Catie appeared to be not having the same good fortune.

Bryce's hearing had been the second in that month, both with good results. They were on a roll. Both Brad Spruce and Bert Hunter had been cleared of any past wrongdoing over the alleged cover-up of war crimes. Major General Ramsay had not fared so well. He had been charged with seven murders of unarmed civilians in Panwa Village, Uruzgan Province and his case was listed for mid-November. Both boys agreed to testify.

Catie's reputation earned another notch as she had scooped the news once again with a front-page story around the nation, one we were not very proud of. The other part of that story had been the conviction of the former army media corps, Gerarde Page, on charges of supplying false evidence in the war crimes investigations. He was dismissed from the Army Reserve, fined $15000 and was being sued by others in civilian courts.

Last Tuesday, Tina had come out of the treatment area to find David, as usual, in the waiting room. They were in time for a relaxed late lunch at Flower Power Nursery and then a final fitting for Tina's outfit for Georgia's wedding the next Saturday at Curzon Hall, Marsfield. She smiled at the thought of tomorrow night's hen's party. Georgia was so excited.

On Wednesday, Tina had called a meeting to wind up 'Task Force Delta'. Once the group were together Tina gave a full summary of their many achievements over the past five months, since forming to investigate the Riley Sampson disappearance. It was a feel good story of triumph over evil. Tina paid special tribute to Nick Pashilidis, Anita Collins and their own Bryce Rixon.

"But before I sign off on our special team, I have one more pleasant duty to announce concerning Detectives Henderson, McHenry and Broadfinger."

Brad, Mike and Georgia looked up enquiringly.

"As from noon this very day, Georgia, you will be Detective Sergeant, Mike and Brad, Inspectors. Congratulations to all three of you, and well deserved."

It is fair to say the meeting broke up on a high, and Georgia couldn't wait to tell he hubby to be. What a wedding present! Mike shook Tina's hand and just smiled. Brad rang Nita with the good news. Nita and the kids had shifted back home over three weeks ago. Their family holiday up north had gone well and there was a real spark back in the marriage. The kids had been delighted. Today's news would help even more.

In the middle of everything going on, Tina had decided to take a big risk. Over the past few months, she had taken a real liking to Rusty Nolan. She realised that he had a foot in both camps and was taking a huge risk. She admired his success and now knew that Rusty had been the key in many major successful police stings over the years.

At Tina's request, Rusty met her for lunch at a small café on Military Road at Neutral Bay. After a few minutes of pleasantries, Rusty asked "So, what do you need from me?"

Tina explained that she was well aware that Rusty was walking a tightrope and was an invaluable contributor to the good guys. "I don't want to know how you do it, or why, but I wanted to tell you that I am in an unusual situation myself. Like you, I am wearing two hats and I am also batting for the right side, but in a questionable way. I need you to accept my word on that with no questions asked.

"I have worked alongside John Palmer for over forty years and trust his judgement implicitly. You are one of the few people that he has one hundred percent faith in, so consider it done. What do you want?" replied Rusty.

They talked. Tina left knowing she had made the right call. She needed help in three places and Rusty may well be able to assist in all of them.

Chapter Thirty-Six

'The 4G Guild' the sign said, and under this 'Home of Geeks, Gadgets, Gigabytes and Gizmos—Global IT and Cyberspace Specialists'.

The new business had been in operation for over a month in Molendinar, at the back of the Gold Coast. General Manager was Brad Spruce. Chairman of the Board was Garth Peterson.

The shop front and factory was ideal for the new team to operate from. Garth had done well.

The finance was arranged and complex purchased in the company name for just under $1.8 million. It was renovated into a reasonable retail office, interview rooms, training room, board/meeting room, canteen and spacious IT/communications centre. The main factory area was a large open area, well equipped as a repair section which would also cover any creative work required. The other plus was that it was a good-sized block of dirt, with room for future expansion.

Brad and Bert had been in charge of both a bomb disposal brigade and a communications unit for many years, and Catie lived and breathed IT. Their skills and knowledge meant they were more than capable when offering IT advice, repairs, upgrades, equipment, and a retail outlet. Garth had set up all the office systems.

They had six full-time staff. Brad, Alvaro and Bert were the factory team. A very bright young mum, Katrina Tee, or KT as she was known, was appointed front of house/receptionist/PA. Two crazy general purpose geeks, Shane Caddy and Kim Knott were mainly responsible for the website, all general enquiries, sales and repairs/upgrades as required. Catie was the only casual employee. Jane Spruce was also on the board.

By day, the operation was all above board but, by night, it was often a workstation for the team. Garth had researched well. There were a few 24/7 operations in this industrial area—just enough to ensure any late night movements did not stand out. But it was quiet enough to offer good security in their bush setting.

KT, Shane and Kim were excellent people and great choices. They were already building a steady business by day, Monday to Friday. All three were totally unaware of the night-shift/weekend warriors' activities. It worked well.

The team had been busy over the past few weeks. Rusty Nolan had certainly delivered for Tina. Not only had he provided Jim Heggarty's hideout address in Surry Hills, but also his silent mobile number and information about the Friday night pizza party he hosted at his hideout. Rusty had also filled in the gaps with valuable information about Joe Iminez, and had followed up Tina's request for more information on Deputy Commissioner Mackay, whose activities had been news to Rusty.

Tina had certainly made the right call there.

Garth, too, had been busy. He had been able to get more intelligence on Aldo Khelner, the senior Immigration Officer keen to see Jumali Qasan deported to Afghanistan.

Tina had seen Khelner's name come up in various mobsters' interviews after the Moriarty Mob were busted and, once, on a statement from the Minister for Immigration, Senator Poplas. None of it was enough to press charges, which was very frustrating for all. The department was aware that all four of his previous deportees had since disappeared and never been seen again, but they lacked concrete proof. All the signs pointed to the fact that not only was Khelner a Taliban sympathiser, but also an active recruiter in Australia.

Alvaro and Bert had been dispatched to Sydney for a week to do some surveillance work. Brad had advised Alvaro to wear a cap, as the blond tufts on top would make him stand out. Bert had been teaching Alvaro the finer points of bomb-making and also how to make covert listening devices. Alvaro was a natural and picked things up very quickly.

Catie was also busy doing what she does best, investigative journalism. Because of her amazing body of news exclusives over the past year, World News Inc wanted to host an invitation-only luncheon for key people, with Catie as the guest speaker. She had to confide in Bob Millman that she was in police witness protection and unavailable.

She also told Bob of her deteriorating health.

Millman had been genuinely concerned on both counts. "Catie, there must be something we can do," he pleaded. "Do you need money or upgraded medical treatments?"

Catie assured him that everything possible was being done and also that she would soon have some more great exclusive stories to submit.

"I don't know where you are getting all these stories from, but you have sure hit the jackpot," Bob said "Please be careful. You are very precious to all of us."

On Sunday afternoon, Catie picked up Tina from Gold Coast Airport. The final team planning meeting was scheduled for seven p.m. at the 4G factory. All of them would be there. As they drove, Tina told Catie all about Georgia's beautiful wedding yesterday. It had been a wonderful day in every way and Tina was so happy for her. "She looked so radiant, she fairly glowed," she said.

Catie then told Tina about Anita's funeral on Friday. Not many there. A sad day, but mum had held up well and her brother, the church minister, was terrific. Tina had looked closely at Catie's face as they drove. She was not her usual self. Her eyes looked flat.

"So, Miss Catie, tell me, what's news on the cancer front?" Tina asked, and immediately saw the result. Catie didn't have to say anything. The mask had dropped.

"Let's stop for coffee," said Tina, and Catie pulled into Amarellos at Varsity Lakes. Over a cuppa, Catie told of the doctor's prognosis. The tumours had grown and secondary cancers had appeared in the lymph glands. It seemed to be spreading fast. The doctor had advised her to expect a decline in her mobility, which would become challenging, and also that she would need lots of rest.

Catie and Tina had discussed palliative care options. Right on six, they purchased takeaway sandwiches and headed for the Molendinar factory.

Brad and Bert were the last to arrive. They had been in Brisbane at an invitation-only veterans' function, celebrating the news that Ramsay had been found guilty and sentenced to life with a minimum prison time of sixteen years. He had glared at them throughout their evidence.

If looks could kill, the boys would both be long gone. Justice had been served.

They pulled into the 4G complex right on 6.45. The mood in the room was subdued. Brad presented the plan for next weekend. It felt like a normal military operation.

"So, it's 'phase one' D Day minus six," he said. "This is going to be a defining week. Here's hoping we have covered all our bases. Friday starts off with Tina's arrest of the Deputy Commissioner. Friday night is Heggarty's pizza party and Saturday should see Mr Iminez going 'fishing' according to all our information. If we achieve our aims, the world will be a much better place on Monday," he concluded as they proceeded to go over the plans step by step.

Garth then said, "Catie, Meg and I will be up here at home-base thinking of the four of you. The work you have done, the creativity and research gives you every chance of success. We will await your coded messages and the results of your intrepid adventures."

Brad, Bert and Alvaro would be driving south on the Wednesday in two vehicles. Tina would be flying back early tomorrow to her 'normal' duties. Brad had the last word before they all broke up.

"Alvaro, you have done really well. Bert's creations are gnomic. That means clever but hard to understand. You have succeeded beyond our wildest expectations. Well done. We all thank you for goading us into this situation. Regardless what happens this weekend, we can all hold our heads up high. We did the best we could. Good luck everyone."

And so the new adventure had begun. 'Phase One' would test them all.

Chapter Thirty-Seven

Tina was nervous. It was Thursday already, D Day minus one. She had spent yesterday at the police pistol shooting range as suggested by Brad 'just in case'. This morning, she had phoned Commissioner Palmer for an appointment and he seemed a little hesitant, not his usual self. He had agreed to meet Tina at three p.m., "but not here" he had said. That was unusual. They agreed to meet at Kirribilli. Being midweek, there was not much traffic, so Tina found she was early. So was the commissioner. He was already seated at a table overlooking the ferry wharf.

"I must say I am a little apprehensive about this," the commissioner said up front. "Rusty rang me yesterday to tell me to expect a call from you that I may not like. That unsettled me. What's happening?"

Tina had gone over this in her mind one hundred times. "After Anita's death, Catie and I went to visit her Mum in Brisbane. She gave us a USB stick, and I would like you to watch it." Tina then turned her iPad around, pressed play, and began sipping her coffee.

Commissioner Palmer watched in silence, taking it all in. His stony face said it all. "Jesus Christ—what next!" he exclaimed at the end. "I had no idea." Right then he felt a failure. Tina then handed him a brief of evidence on Kel Mackay obtained from a number of sources. "This won't make you feel any better," she said.

John Palmer read them. He was breathing slowly. "When I think of some of the classified intelligence I have given Kel, I feel sick knowing now where it went. This answers a lot of nagging questions I have had for a while." He was far from happy.

Tina then advised the commissioner that Mackay was on afternoon shift tomorrow and asked could she do the arrest herself. "I just want to see the look on his face," she said.

"We'll do it together," said the commissioner. "I'll call him for a 3.15 p.m. meeting to make sure he is in the office when we strike at three. There are things I need to have in place before we do it. We need to have him well under cover before Joe Iminez gets wind of it, and by the sound of it that will be within seconds of it happening. I'll see if I can get phone taps in place. We may get a few more rats," he said sourly.

Tina then handed him a second brief—this one on Iminez. "While you are in the mood, you'd better read this as well," she said. John Palmer took it all in and looked at Tina. "I've no idea where you are getting all this. Is your back covered?" he asked, concerned.

"I'm in a good place, Sir. Just happy to be getting square for the Anitas, Nicks and Rixons of this world," Tina replied.

"Well, it finally looks like Mr Iminez will be spending a lot of time as a guest of Her Majesty. I just hope we can make it stick this time. When do you propose to move on him? It will sure rock the socialite boat."

"Early next week," Tina lied. "We will have all the paperwork and warrants processed on Monday/ Tuesday and hope he doesn't get wind of it. He will be nervous with Mackay in custody."

"You know, Tina, I joined the force nearly forty years ago hoping to do some good. We've achieved more in the last eight weeks than the previous thirty-nine years and seven months," said the commissioner, "and now we have more happening."

He was brightening up and went on. "On another matter, Olga Sarmiento's speaking tour is now confirmed. Mid November, Brisbane, Sydney and Melbourne. It will be announced late next week. How do you want to handle it?"

Tina smiled. "That is wonderful news. Alvaro has asked me when it would be safe to go home as Bernardo. He's prepared to take the risk. What do you think?" she asked.

"I think we should get Alvaro together with Deputy Commissioner Alan MacDonald in Canberra. Together they can nut out the best plan," the commissioner replied. "Better still, do it in my office. I would love to meet him."

"Great. I'll get onto it this afternoon. Thanks," said Tina.

They left the café just after four. Tina rang Alvaro with the news. He was overjoyed.

She drove back to Chatswood to brief Mike on the Kel Mackay case and then home for dinner and a long discussion with David. Playing a double agent's role was taking its toll on her.

Chapter Thirty-Eight

Friday started like any ordinary day, but that would change.

Tina left Chatswood just before two p.m., as she wanted to be early at Day St HQ. She had all the paperwork she needed to lay charges. She also had butterflies in her stomach.

Meantime Brad, Bert and Alvaro were also in Sydney and they, too, were preparing for a big night. They, too, were nervous.

Tina met with Commissioner Palmer right on three p.m. Shortly after, they walked down the corridor to Deputy Commissioner Mackay's office and entered without knocking. Kel Mackay was in discussion with a junior police officer. He looked up, puzzled.

"What's going on?" he demanded.

The commissioner produced an iPad and said "Kel, I'd like you to watch this." He pressed the play arrow and watched as Mackay started to go very pale. His hands suddenly moved quickly to his top drawer and came up holding his service revolver.

Tina was quicker. Brad had made her unbutton the flap and she was ready. It was standard army procedure.

The two shots were almost simultaneous. Mackay's face was contorted as he slid lifelessly from his chair. The glass wall behind Tina smashed into millions of pieces, but the shot itself had just missed her. For a moment in time everyone stood still in total disbelief, then pandemonium broke out in police headquarters.

It took a few seconds to realise no one had been hit by Mackay's bullet. Tina had immediately grabbed his gun, just in case, before dialling triple zero for an ambulance. Staff came running from everywhere staring in disbelief. They began CPR on the deputy commissioner, but to no avail.

Tina began to shake. The realisation that she had just shot and killed a colleague was sinking in. She felt unsteady. The commissioner saw this and recommended she take away the junior constable who was in Mackay's office and record his statement. This gave Tina something to do and allowed her to take her mind off what just happened. She switched into police mode immediately. She soon established the young constable was being reprimanded for a minor breach of police discipline. Tina explained to him the circumstances behind what had just happened and the reasons why she and the commissioner were about to arrest Mackay. She then recorded his statement on what had happened in the room. The young policeman was amazed at her apparent calmness and strength. Little did he know!

Tina was just back in the commissioner's office when her phone vibrated. It was Mike.

"Shit, Boss. What happened? We've just heard!"

Tina responded that she was okay and would call back in five minutes or so.

The commissioner was in the middle of thanking her for saving their lives when a constable stuck his head in. "Sorry, Commissioner, thought you'd want to know. Joe Iminez is already aware of what happened and Detective Noel Sunberry has just been arrested. The phone tap worked. We are charging him now," he reported.

"Bloody Sunberry. Never liked him," snorted the commissioner, smugly happy that his plan had worked but pissed off that the ship had yet another senior rat.

Around five p.m., and after she had phoned Catie, Tina arrived back at Chatswood. She called her key people in and briefed them on what had transpired at Day Street. They could see she was still genuinely upset by proceedings. When the briefing was over, Mike asked, "Hey, Super, it's been a big day. How about a few beers and dinner with us?"

"Gladly," Tina replied smiling. Perfect! She needed both the company and an alibi. All eight headed out the door and down to the Chatswood RSL club for dinner.

Chapter Thirty-Nine

"**S**urry Pizza," came the bored voice over the radio in the van parked outside Jim Heggarty's hideout. The three men listened as the delivery order was placed for three large pizzas.

"Okay. About twenty-five to thirty minutes, Mr Brown. That will be $48. Will it be cash or credit card?" asked the pizza man.

"Cash," came the reply from inside the house, and they both hung up.

Alvaro and Brad slowly sauntered to the car parked just down the road and drove to Surry Pizza, just four blocks away. Bert stayed in the van listening. So far, so good.

About ten minutes later Alvaro, cap on, walked into the pizza shop and announced he was here to pick up an order for Brown. Delivery was not required now, as they were heading out to visit friends. He gave the address, listed the pizzas to the cashier and paid. Some five minutes later, the order was ready and Alvaro asked if he could buy an empty pizza box.

"You can have one. We saved on the delivery charge," said the cashier.

Brad drove back to Heggarty's and parked just across the road. They quickly and silently took the pizzas inside the van and got to work before Brad got out, walked through the gate and rang the doorbell. A man opened the door to one of the biggest pizza delivery guys he had ever seen. He paid Brad $50 and told him to keep the change.

"Thanks, Mr Brown," said Brad and walked back to the car and drove off at the same time as the van.

Both vehicles had only gone about 200 metres when they heard a very loud explosion. They kept driving towards Rushcutters Bay and their next rendezvous.

Twenty minutes later, three men sat in silence in the waterfront park in Neild Avenue sharing the third pizza. It was only lukewarm, and they weren't all that hungry. Two of them then quietly changed into wet suits while Alvaro inflated the rubber duck. They all then loaded equipment onto the vessel and carried it to the water's edge, where Brad and Bert rowed off quietly into the night. They didn't have far to go.

The next morning, Saturday, dawned and showed Sydney Harbour at her sparkling best. Not a breath of wind, clear blue skies and the sun's rays beaming down on the crystal-clear blue water of Rushcutters Bay. It couldn't get better.

Just before nine a.m., Joe Iminez and his two compatriots arrived at nearby New Beach Road and boarded a water taxi waiting to take them and their supplies out to the *Spirit of Flight*, Iminez's magnificent power yacht with a spectacular fly bridge. The three men loaded the supplies, boarded the boat and paid the water taxi, then began unpacking their gear ready for what looked like a great fishing day on the harbour.

In fact, they were going out of the heads for a rendezvous out at sea. It was the perfect day for a special delivery.

A few minutes later, everything was stowed or tied down. Iminez climbed the few stairs to the fly bridge, inserted and turned the keys and pressed the start button. There was an instant massive explosion. Bits of boat, rigging, flames and smoke were blown high into the air. The peace and quiet of the morning was shattered, and burning bits began landing all around the marina and surrounding boats. There would be no rendezvous at sea today and no fishing ever again for these three sailors. The burning hull was sinking quickly as the sirens started.

This was one for Anita.

At that precise moment, Tina was enjoying a shampoo, cut and blow-dry at her normal Epping hairdressers. Brad, Bert and Alvaro were enjoying brunch at The Paddock Bakery at Miami on the Gold Coast, where they were well known and had pre-booked the table under Brad's name. The three boys had driven back overnight. Both Tina and Brad kept their receipts with date and time on them. Great alibis all round.

Phase one of their plan was complete.

Chapter Forty

"**A**lvaro, I would like you to meet Commissioner Palmer and Federal Police Force Deputy Commissioner MacDonald."

Tina conducted the introductions. A few pleasantries were exchanged and both men thanked Alvaro for his valuable undercover work before Tina said, "These two gentlemen are the ones who have kept you safe, paid the bills and, more importantly, organised your exchange of letters and Olga's forthcoming speaking tour, so you can be completely open with them on anything and everything. I would like you to tell your story, from a childhood in Bogota." Tina had prepared Alvaro for this moment and taught him a few boundaries. He was a good student.

Alvaro had thanked both men from the bottom of his heart for what they had done for him. He then went back to his early days and told the same tale as he had at Garth's barbecue. He left nothing out and pushed the point that his remaining family were still fighting organised crime and the cartels in Colombia.

"Given the success of your international operations over the past few weeks, I am sure they are somewhat safer now, so I again say thank you, from me and also Colombia." Alvaro went on, "But, my real dream is to return to Colombia as Bernardo and re-join my family for a period, and then come back to Australia with my immediate family. This is a wonderful country to give our two adult children a good future," Alvaro continued.

An hour later, the meeting broke up with handshakes and smiles all round. They had covered a whole range of risks and current gang activities. Alvaro was amazed at Alan MacDonald's knowledge of Colombian activities and his extensive list of contacts. He even knew some of Alvaro's extended family. They also discussed Alvaro's hoped-for return and all the risks involved.

They finished by going over Olga's and the children's Australian itinerary. Alvaro was in a buoyant mood as they left and went down to the basement carpark to the black SUV with dark tinted windows.

Chapter Forty-One

Black ties and stylish evening gowns strolled along the red carpet as VIP guests arrived at the Sydney International Convention Centre for the Annual Walkley Gala Dinner and Awards.

Top journalists and photographers from all over the nation were joined by senior media executives, major corporate partners and industry giants to recognise and reward excellence in journalism. It was their night of nights, the Australian equivalent of the American Pulitzer Prize. Over sixteen-hundred attendees were being ushered to their elaborately decorated tables of ten.

The World News Inc Australia table was set between BHP Billiton and Qantas, and there was an element of confidence in their group, as they had nominated finalists in five categories. Catie Lanyon was the star of her table with two nominations, the first for news reports and the second for excellence in journalism. Win or lose, it didn't matter to Catie. It was recognition enough to be a finalist as judged by a panel of eminent independent journalists and photographers from around the globe—a real honour.

Catie was just happy to be there with her colleagues. Coming along the red carpet with her new 'attachment' was a bit of a challenge. It was unusual to see such a strikingly beautiful young woman with a walking frame, but now she was seated all was fine and she just wanted to soak up the atmosphere and enjoy herself.

The dinner, bands, dancers and artists were all world-class, and the shows were interspersed with the presentation of the thirty-three Walkley's—a long night.

It was nearing eleven p.m. when the M.C. advised they were about to announce the final four, and most prestigious, awards. The World News Inc team were already celebrating, with one major award and one highly commended. Bob Millman was in a great mood.

The buzz in the room ceased as the M.C. announced, "The winner of the Walkley Award for best news report," he paused, "her exposure of the world illegal arms-trade network, is Catie Lanyon from World News Inc!"

The crowd erupted.

It was a popular choice. Catie needed assistance to mount the stairs and, when they saw the walking frame, many of her colleagues realised for the first time that she had serious health issues.

A tearful Catie thanked her own colleagues for their support and encouragement in what had been a challenging year on a number of fronts. She spoke of the difficulties encountered by journalists protecting sources and staying within the boundaries of Draconian and uncertain media laws that seemed to be set up mainly to protect incompetent politicians. The sixteen-hundred guests gave her a loud and appreciative send off.

"Congratulations, Catie. That will be a hard act to follow," said the M.C. He then proceeded to reveal the winner of the 'Photographer of the Year Award', which went to a freelance fellow from the Gippsland area for his images from the devastating bush fires that had destroyed a lot of Victoria and, indeed, much of the country over last summer. He had thanked the climate change deniers. "Without you, I could never have taken these photos." The crowd loved it.

Back at the microphone, the MC warmed up. "And now, Ladies and Gentlemen, for the penultimate award of the evening—the award for 'Excellence in Journalism'. For amazing coverage exposing worldwide-drug cartels and criminal organisations, welcome back to the stage... Catie Lanyon from World News Inc."

Catie rose to instant and spontaneous loud applause as she made her way, with assistance, slowly up the stairs onto the stage. She had not been expecting this.

This time Catie acknowledged the contribution of her family and close friends. She spoke of the many late nights and frustrating stonewalls but also the tremendous sense of satisfaction and fulfilment when evil was exposed.

Once again, she received a huge ovation as she made her way

slowly back to her table, talking to many well-wishers as she went. The unobtrusive extra plain-clothes police and security put in place to protect Catie on the night were feeling nervous with all her success and were sending reports to their colleagues in the crowd outside.

"Ladies and Gentlemen, we are now at the major award of the year, Australian journalism's highest honour—The Gold Walkley Award. I have much pleasure in welcoming our Prime Minister, Isla Rose, to the stage to announce the winner and make the presentation."

The crowd gave an appreciative round of applause for their popular P.M.

The crowd was hushed as the PM opened the envelope. All the night's previous category winners were on edge. Her eyes lit up as she read the name. "Ladies and Gentlemen, for deep and sustained investigative journalism at its best, this year's winner is…. Catie Lanyon."

The Walkleys had never experienced such an explosive response to their prize award. All sixteen-hundred were on their feet, stamping and clapping and yelling for many minutes. Catie was really overwhelmed at this totally unexpected honour. She ascended the stairs for the final time, accepted the award from Prime Minister Rose and turned to the lectern.

Catie waited for the room to retake their seats. They were ready to listen.

"My friends, this has come as a huge surprise and I am humbled beyond words. Sadly, barring a miracle, I am told this will be my last time at this wonderful night." She gulped and 1600 people fell into stunned silence.

"Let me just say that our country is worth fighting for and the genuine freedom of the press is paramount to the success of our future. Evil and incompetence must be exposed at all levels and we are the ones who must continue to fight for good and right. There are eight people to whom we all owe a massive debt for my stories this year. Three are dead, murdered by the organised criminals we exposed."

"The other five know who they are, and I just pray those evil bastards and their protectors never find out. But we all know the risks and are happy to take them for the betterment of Australia and beyond.

I dedicate this award to the person who inspired me to take up this challenge. I give you Juanita Neilsen," she concluded, with her award held high and tears flowing down both cheeks.

The roof of the convention centre nearly lifted off.

Chapter Forty-Two

This was the first time the whole team had been seen in public and also Alvaro's first time in Canberra. They were trying to be as inconspicuous as possible and were somewhat slowed down because of Catie's latest accessory—the wheelchair. It was the best available, sourced and purchased by Garth, who was pushing it now up the Parliament house ramp.

Tina, Brad, Alvaro and Bert were in deep conversation about the forthcoming meeting and, also, this morning's visit to the impressive Australian War Memorial Museum. The six of them were ushered into a private dining annexe and seated in preparation for lunch and to hear answers to their various discussion points. Right on time, the other six walked in, led by Prime Minister Isla Rose. After the final six were seated, the Prime Minister spoke.

"Garth, I will get you to introduce your group shortly but first I would like to introduce my party and I must say, in all my years I have never hosted such a diverse group and I am honoured to be here. On my left, Deputy Commissioner of the Australian Federal Police Force, Alan MacDonald. Next to him is General David Ambleside, head of the Australian Defence Force." The General nodded. "And then Commissioner of the NSW Police Force John Palmer. And I am pleased to say, the Columbian Ambassador to Australia, General Abut Du Gorez, has been able to join us."

The general smiled at everyone and nodded to Alvaro who was seated next to him.

"And finally, the Director of Home Affairs and Immigration, Dr Bridget Smythe, and I am Isla Rose," said the Prime Minister. "Now I ask my old friend Garth Peterson to introduce our other VIP guests."

Garth responded with an appropriate thank you to the PM and all her party, then introduced himself and his team.

For the next twenty minutes or so there was general banter around the room and across the table as a light lunch was served followed by tea, coffee and juices, and then Prime Minister Rose tapped her glass and took the floor.

"Okay, firstly I just want to put on record our nation's thanks to all six of you for whatever role you each played in the recent Australian and Colombian Drug Cartel dismantling, the exposure of the illegal Middle East arms-trade networks and your contribution to the Australia War Crimes Enquiry.

"Not only have they been incredibly successful outcomes but also the world is now a much better and safer place and, I am led to believe, we owe it all to you. So, thank you. *Thank you*."

There were general murmurs of assent around the room.

"Next up, I want to cover some specific points raised by Garth in a phone call to me some weeks ago and the later written submissions. I am sure you are all aware that there has been a tremendous amount of behind-the-scenes negotiations and investigations taking place and I hope you are happy with the results. Before I start, can I say that I am normally guarded by what I say in the presence of a feared investigative journalist such as Catie Lanyon, but not today. Catie, you are to be congratulated on your remarkably accurate and responsible in-depth reporting on these sensitive matters."

Catie beamed and nodded graciously

"We all congratulate you for scooping the pool—pardon the pun— at the Walkley Awards." Isla smiled and Catie blushed.

"So, on the matter of the Mates 4 Mates submission, I am pleased to announce today that $3.5 million has been placed in next year's budgets to allow for the expansion of this terrific organisation doing so much for our returned service personnel."

Brad and Bert smiled at each other. They knew what a difference this would make. It was already worth the trip.

"On the matter of Jumali Qasan, I can confirm today that one of our Department of Immigration senior staff, Aldo Khelner, has been suspended pending an investigation into a number of allegations. Further, in recognition of his years of risk taking and loyal service,

Jumali and his family will be granted permanent residency in Australia with the view to full citizenship in the years ahead."

There was a visible sigh of relief from many in the room. They almost clapped. The two soldiers were ecstatic.

"Now to the matter of Bernardo Rodriguez Sarmiento. This has been a real challenge, but with fantastic assistance from General Du Gorez, we have been able to find a way forward." Prime Minister Rose looked directly at Alvaro. "You and your family have been to hell and back for many, many years. Your amazing story of survival and your perseverance and personal contribution to a better world will, hopefully, be a lesson for the faint hearted."

I can announce today the approval of your permanent residency status in Australia plus our joint plan to send you home to Colombia, carrying a Colombian diplomatic passport, with your wife Olga and your two children, following her speaking tour later this month." She looked directly at Alvaro. "Bernardo, as with the rest of your courageous family, your life will always be at risk. However, between the Colombian authorities and our own Federal and State Police here in Australia, we will be doing all in our power to keep you and your family safe at all times. We all agree that the world needs more Sarmientos."

Alvaro was trying hard to hold it all together, but the tears on both cheeks gave him away. His mind flashed back to his late friend Nick. He wished he could see all this and the great good that had come out of his introduction to Tina. He could not believe how his life could turn around so quickly and positively in just a few short months.

Most of those present were looking at either the ceiling or the floor trying to mask their own emotions.

Prime Minister Rose went on, "I have two more announcements to make in relation to these events over and above those on the agenda. Firstly, the appointment of Head of Security at NSW Parliament House. Premier Johnson will announce tomorrow that this role will be offered to retired NSW Police Sergeant Bryce Rixon."

Tina nearly fell off her chair. She looked straight at Commissioner Palmer, who was wearing a knowing smile.

"And finally," the PM went on, "closer to home. As most of you know Commissioner Kendall of our Australian Federal Police Force is retiring in January, and it is my pleasant duty to announce today that his replacement will be current Deputy Commissioner Alan MacDonald, and we all know our beloved country will remain in safe hands."

There was spontaneous applause all around the room. Most were happy to be releasing pent-up emotions from everything announced. Alan MacDonald just smiled and nodded appreciatively.

Half-an-hour later, twelve happy people left the plush dining room annexe.

"If only they all finished this way," lamented the PM as she waved goodbye.

The team of six headed straight to the airport for the flight to Brisbane.

Phase one had been completed—with bonuses.

Chapter Forty-Three

There people sat anxiously in the Coffee Club on the arrivals deck at Brisbane International Airport intently looking at the screens showing incoming flights. Watching passengers coming down the chute towards the exit gate, they did not even notice the extra plain-clothes police and security in the terminal.

Suddenly, Alvaro stiffened. There they were: Olga, Rodriguez and Zarla, in the tunnel. Brad, Bert and Alvaro moved as one towards the exit doors. Olga spotted Alvaro instantly and came running, with Rodriguez pushing the trolley and Zarla speeding up, trying to keep pace.

Everyone watching realised this was a reunion years in the making. The four of them hugged, talking excitedly and laughing. Tears flowed, but there were also smiles all around. Finally, Alvaro introduced his family to Brad and Bert, who escorted them out of the terminal to the car park where they loaded the luggage into the eight-seater people mover with the 4G logo on each side. They were soon on their way to the Gold Coast, just as the sun was setting over the Brisbane River and Gateway Bridge.

Brad drove, with Bert in the front seat. They understood not one word of the conversation, except when Alvaro or Olga spoke to them. The boys were surprised that Olga spoke excellent English, one of five languages she speaks fluently. Both Rodriguez and Zarla had only a smattering of school-styled English language.

Olga's first public presentation was in Brisbane the following Friday, so they had four days to relax and get over the dreaded jet lag and get to know each other all over again.

The family were in awe of their apartment. Brad and Bert took the bags in, then left. Once again, security was quietly in place both on the twenty-fifth floor and also downstairs.

Next morning, Alvaro took his family to visit Catie, whose health had declined markedly over the past few weeks. She was in bed at her mother's unit. She was not well.

Olga and Catie hit it off instantly. They chatted for quite a while, enjoying tea and scones on the balcony overlooking the lake. Rodriguez and Zarla could not get over the beautiful lorikeet parrots that they could hand feed. They loved the screeching sulphur-crested cockatoos. Later, the family drove to Alvaro's canal-front unit where they fished and swam, just enjoying the privacy and their own company. Tomorrow they were heading to Sea World and looking forward to more exciting discoveries.

On Wednesday, Tina flew in from Sydney and went straight to Catie, who was not faring well. She told Tina she thought her hospital admission was nearing. That night, Brad and Jane, Bert and Nita Hunter, Tina and David joined the four Sarmientos in Garth's and Meg's sub-penthouse for a wonderful barbecue. Rodriguez and Zarla were super impressed, with both the apartment itself and the pool, as well as the food.

Sadly, Catie had been unable to join them, but her name kept cropping up as Alvaro recounted many of his adventures over the past few months. Even the teenagers were included, as every now and again either Alvaro or Olga would translate the tale. They loved it. A great night was had by all. The Spruces and Hunters left first, as the boys were driving south early tomorrow.

Alvaro kept everyone entertained with his stories of what he was going to do when he arrived back on Colombian soil in a few weeks' time. He couldn't wait! Olga picked him up at one point, saying some of his ideas were way over the family budget limits. Garth quietly told her that was not going to be an issue. The evening finished around eleven p.m., with everyone in great spirits.

Chapter Forty-Four

Tina and David were woken at dawn the next morning with a call from Catie's mum. Catie had become gravely ill overnight. She had called an ambulance around four a.m. Catie was taken to Gold Coast Private Hospital and was immediately admitted to the intensive care unit. They decided to shower, dress and head to the hospice after a light breakfast

The sun was rising as Brad and Bert crossed the border travelling north, just south of Warwick. They would be home in two hours. Their trip to the nation's capital had been quick and quiet. They had been previously advised that Aldo Khelmer could likely get off, as the evidence was all circumstantial at this point.

The six a.m. news came on, and the radio reported the death of a suspended Department of Immigration official in Canberra who had links to both the Taliban and the Crown Prince of Saudi Arabia. He had died overnight as a result of an apparent car bomb. Police were investigating.

Mission accomplished. Phase two had begun.

The boys just smiled. This was much better than Afghanistan, because they knew that the enemy—every target—was truly evil. Jumali would never know what they had done and why, but he would have been proud of them. It was a pity they hadn't done it sooner. More decent lives would have been saved.

As the sun was setting later that day, Tina, Garth, Alvaro, Brad and Bert met at the 4G factory. The 4G legitimate operation was flourishing. Shane, Kim and KT were doing a brilliant job and business was booming, so much so they had put on two extra full-time geeks. One took Catie's part-time role and the other helped handle the increasing business. Real money was pouring in.

Everyone present was extremely worried about Catie and her failing health. Tina reported on their visit this morning. They all decided to head to the hospice following their meeting.

For the first time, the team did a complete debrief on all of their Phase One activities in Surry Hills and Rushcutters Bay, and on the death of Kel Mackay during his attempted arrest. They also discussed both the success of the Prime Minister's luncheon and Catie's Walkley Awards clean up. The boys then briefly told them about the successful start of phase two and the Canberra operation.

"Alvaro, whatever you started, we are already way in front of anything I thought we would achieve by now, so thank you," said Garth. "Here's hoping we continue to do well, for Catie's sake. We have all gone into this with our eyes open and are happy to take the risks involved, regardless of our health challenges."

Alvaro still hadn't come down to earth. His week just kept getting better. Olga and their children were very keen to return and live in Australia. They were having a ball. All three speaking engagements were now complete sell-outs, and Brisbane had already been staged and really well-received and critiqued. They were heading home to Colombia in just two weeks, and were really looking forward to it.

Just as the meeting was breaking up, Garth said, "Before we go, I just wanted to tell you that, following a settlement today, all the real estate and buildings are now unencumbered and completely owned by the 4G company, with Brad and Bert as the only shareholders. Congratulations lads. You deserve every bit of it."

The boys were gob smacked. This was beyond anything they ever thought possible in their lives. Tina and Alvaro were very happy for them.

They all left to visit Catie. On arrival, it was obvious she had completely succumbed to this evil cancer. She was very pale and gaunt and was having trouble communicating. Garth and Tina felt a tad guilty, as both their reports had been encouraging.

Brad went through all the news about their success in Sydney and the wash up of phase one. He also advised that phase two was already underway and talked about events in Canberra overnight.

Catie sparked up immediately with all this news. She was the only one in the room smiling. She tried to lift their spirits.

"Very soon I will be sipping champagne with Anita and Nick and boasting about my Walkley Awards," she sparkled. "In my wildest dreams, I could never have imagined we could do so much good for so many people in such a short time. All six of us can thank our lucky stars. I can never thank you enough. You are the best friends anyone could ever ask for. I want to let you know, I filed my final story this afternoon with an embargo on it until Alvaro and Olga leave for Colombia. It is my finest work ever and I am very proud of it, as I am of all of you. Whatever happens from now on, you must continue!" With that, she closed her eyes. It was time to rest.

Everyone leant over and kissed Catie goodbye. She was still smiling as they left.

CHAPTER FORTY-FIVE

It was just before ten a.m. on a crisp but bright Wednesday morning in Brisbane as Brad and Jane, Alvaro, Olga and their children, Garth and Meg, Tina and David, and Bert and Nita all filed past the hearse and down to the grave site to say their final goodbye to Catie. There was a huge crowd. Many hundreds of mourners attended an uplifting service.

At exactly that time, at Parramatta in Sydney, a black SUV was parked some three-hundred metres from the Police HQ. No one was taking any notice of the uniformed policeman sitting in the driver's seat, phone in hand. There was a sudden massive explosion and the Police HQ seemed to burst into a million flying pieces. Debris flew hundreds of feet in the air and seemed to hang there before crashing back to earth over a large area as the sonic boom echoed along the street.

It was all captured on the phone video the driver held up after he had pressed 'Send'. *The godfather will be happy*, he thought, as he pulled out of the parking spot for the short drive to the bomb site. He came to a sudden stop and rushed out of the vehicle and up the stairs in an apparent attempt to rescue his colleagues trapped in the fire and rubble. There were dead and injured lying everywhere and a great deal of panic amongst the confusion.

"I am the resurrection and the life, saith the Lord.

He that believeth in me, though he were dead, yet shall he live.

And whoever liveth and believeth in me, shall never die."

The Minister continued as Catie's casket was lowered into the grave. "In the name of Our Lord Jesus Christ, crucified and risen, we commend to God's merciful care, Catherine Elizabeth Lanyon.

"'Earth to Earth, Dust to Dust, Ashes to Ashes. Blessed are the dead'."

And then there were five.

As the five walked away tearfully from the grave site, uphill towards the Teahouse, Tina caught sight of Mike Broadfinger walking briskly down to her. He looked terrible. Tina approached him, fearing the worst.

"What's up Mike?" she asked.

"Sorry, Boss. We just heard there has been a major bomb blast at Parramatta Police HQ," Mike whispered. "They are saying up to ten police and civilians have been killed, and it seems Inspector Sward is one of them."

Tina froze on the spot.

Brad came straight over and grabbed Tina's arm, as it looked like she was about to faint. "Tina, what's wrong?"

Tina looked the man-mountain in the eye and spoke with strong resolve.

"We've still got work to do. It's not over yet."

ACKNOWLEDGMENTS AND THANKS

To realise any dream takes a team effort, and I would like to thank all those who helped in so many ways:

To Smithy, for all her help and encouragement.

Jim K and Lorraine C. They sure did the hard yards.

To Patrick W—he's got us covered!

And for all the invaluable research, reference works and inspiration, I acknowledge Spiro, Mike B, Honkey, Sprabbit, Catie L, John P, Jaqui L, Kelly, GP, Bert H, Nick E, Terry McC, Brian K, Katherine C and Alison F.

The story may be all fiction, but writing it it was a lot of fun. Together we did it, and the results are on the shelf.

About the Author

Lance enjoyed the response from publishing his memoirs so much so that it convinced him to start working on his long held ambition to write a series of fictional crime thrillers.

During his teenage years, driving tow trucks and repossessing in Sydney, he mixed in a world of colourful, sometimes dangerous, characters. Later, travelling the world as a young man, he joined the London Fire Brigade, worked as an interpreter in Paris, a hospital aide in Holland, and learned the fine art of dishwashing in Greece and Germany... experiencing the best and worst of many things in life with all its diversity

Back home, he rejoined the Fire Brigade in Sydney's Kings Cross, then, in his mid 20s —over 50 years ago now—he met and married his gorgeous wife, Helen, whilst working on Queensland's Whitsunday Islands. He also fell in love with Mother Nature and the beauty, marine life and colours of the Great Barrier Reef.

Together he and Helen raised three children and now have seven much-loved grandchildren living around the world.

Through his various achievements—Shire President, the bicentennial Advance Australia Award, his Order of Australia and his 20 years working with the Oncology kids at Camperdown and later Westmead Children's Hospital, he saw the very best and worst, highs and lows of life. All this was the perfect recipe for a 'good versus evil' novel.

It was during his stage career he got the idea of harnessing both his creative side and his imagination with the many characters and challenges he had experienced along the way: a fantasy to make the world a safer and nicer place to live. Now, you too can go on this journey."